# Sea Glass

By

**Julie Ann Rees**

**Black Bee Books Ltd.**

First Published in Great Britain in 2025 by
Black Bee Books Ltd
Bryn Heulog
Talley
Llandeilo
Wales SA19 7YH
Copyright © Julie Ann Rees 2025

The moral right of the author has been asserted.

All rights reserved.

Without limiting the rights under copyright reserved above, no part of this publication may be reproduced, stored in or introduced into a retrieval system, or transmitted in any form or by any means (electronic, mechanical, photocopying, recording or otherwise), without the prior written permission of both the copyright owner and the above publisher of the work.

This book is a work of fiction. Names, places, characters and locations are used fictitiously and any resemblance to actual persons, living or dead, is purely coincidental and a product of the author's creativity.

Cover Image © E.Autumn
Cover Design © Huw Francis

ISBN: 978-1-913853-14-3 (Paperback)
ISBN: 978-1-913853-15-0 (eBook)
Printed and bound in Great Britain by Clays Ltd, Elcograf S.p.A

www.blackbeebooks.wales

# Acknowledgements

To my father, thanks Dad for telling me scary stories when Mam didn't know. Your description and drawing of *The Thing from Another World* stayed with me, shaping my imagination and awakening my mind to the uncanny and all things horror;

To my mother, thanks for always being there when I woke screaming from nightmares. Even when, once, I ran so fast out of my bedroom after a particularly terrifying dream, we collided, and I broke your toe; even in pain, you still tucked me back in (even if a little angrily);

To my sister, thanks Sha for making me do the Ouija board when I was terrified and for never failing to frighten me when we were kids. I'll never forget about 'Teddy's God' and that hideous burnt, scarred teddy bear, who never left your side as a child (you know what I'm referring to);

To my daughter, thanks for designing this book's fantastic front cover, and for being the best horror film companion ever. Whilst I shook and trembled in fear all night with images of the film we'd watched imprinted on my brain, you slept like a log – muttering in your sleep like a being possessed – maximising my terror. Friday nights will always mean horror night;

To all the cats and hamsters, that I made sleep in my room over the years, who no doubt protected me from the eldritch realms and beings of the demonic Other World always attempting to invade my bedroom. You guys kept me safe. Even though it is pussy cat Griffin's job these days, I know he is supported by you all, like little orbs of light warriors. I thank you;

Finally, I thank my childhood home, for being the scariest, coldest, eeriest, yet spine chillingly fabulous, haunted house a future horror writer could grow up in. Standing tall and sinister (before the pretty green trim was added around your windows), and dating from the year 1746, with your Welsh name translating to 'Blue Marsh', *Hill House* has nothing on you.

# Dedication

For my daughter

# Foreword by Carly Holmes

I first met Julie Ann around a decade ago when I was working at Lampeter University offering writing surgeries to the students. She brought me a range of work over the different sessions: fragments of memoir, short stories, and outlines for longer pieces of fiction. Her writing, both in form and subject, chimed with me immediately. This was a writer and reader who shared my own fascination for the darker side of life, a mutual love for the natural world around us, and a similar slant approach to narrative.

We kept in touch after my contract with the university ended and I was thrilled to see *Paper Horses*, her brave, wise and deeply thoughtful memoir about surviving coercive control, published in 2022. Blending fairy-tale tropes with the grim reality of her situation, this debut publication showed a writer who had already found her voice and her own unconventional style, and had the confidence to be true to both.

Some of the stories in this collection I'm already familiar with from previous publications, and some I'm reading for the very first time. Lines leap out from the pages: landscapes *like blood and bone*; eyes *like cherry stones*; trees that live on *like sweet honey*, reincarnated as the frames of houses. The rich descriptive language threads through each story like a necklace of jewels.

The stories themselves range widely, and wildly. There are grieving mothers and abused wives; confused, furious, vengeful humans and spirits; worlds that tilt and morph from one reality to another. Magic realism, folk horror, fairy tale and fantasy: all can be found in *Sea Glass*.

It has been and will continue to be a real pleasure following Julie Ann's writing career, from those early days and tentative early drafts, to these mature, imaginative and rounded stories, written by a person whose love for the written word and the magic of storytelling shines through on every page.

# Contents

| | |
|---|---|
| The Fall of Pan | 1 |
| Jack and the Juniper Tree | 5 |
| The Sleeping Giant | 15 |
| The Cloying Scent of Apples | 22 |
| The Damson Tree | 31 |
| Transcending | 33 |
| Sea Glass | 42 |
| The Grundylow | 49 |
| Alderwood | 56 |
| Poor ole Annie | 69 |
| Sacks | 73 |
| Where the Bad Wind Blows | 83 |
| Through the Yellow Wallpaper | 92 |
| Whispering Poplars | 100 |
| Why Don't You Turn Round and Look at Me? | 110 |
| Heart and Home | 119 |
| Weep Willow Weep | 127 |
| The Islanders | 134 |
| Hunted | 138 |
| My Spirit and I | 142 |
| My Baby He Ate Me | 148 |
| Swine | 155 |
| About the author | 161 |

# The Fall of Pan

It was always in the hazel grove I heard him, whimpering softly like a newborn lamb. I walked this way often, taking in the view that carved across the land, changing and morphing from hill to crag, dale to wood and patchwork fields to finally the cold bleak sea where the power station coughed its foul breath. A smattering of rooftops rose up the valley like an invasion to meet the farms that dotted the lower hills.

It was early spring and the trees were budding, returning to life after winter's death. Dark green moss furred the trunks and hung from the limbs as lichen sprouted, pale and frosted silver, over the branches. The scent of earth filled my lungs as, breathing deeply, my boots disturbed the leafy mulch, and soft black pressed through the crisp rusted woodland floor.

It came again, a whimper, and a small movement flitted behind the mossy trunks. I called out, following my line of sight to where the movement occurred. As I stared I noticed tiny fingertips gripping either side of a narrow trunk. Bony and twig-like they unfurled and pulled sharply away. Approaching slowly, I begun to hum a tune, an old folk song of mist and mountain tops. Turning softly my gaze reached behind the tree and stared down into tangled bramble and bracken.

A small flash of fur, brown and tattered, scrabbled with little hands clutching and burrowing into the moss. A head turned away cowering and shook as the whimpers increased. I smoothed the hunched and shuddering shoulders, cold and scabby to the touch. My hand recoiled and I flushed with embarrassment. The shaggy body contorted into misshapen legs, twisted and swollen, where little hooves, cloven and cracked, kicked at the dirt.

He was smaller and weaker than last time. His head looked up from a spine of neck, wobbling, the once-mighty horns broken and shrunken. I sat and pulled off my rucksack, handing him an apple, a Cox's from the tree in my garden. Crooked fingers reached and took whilst chipped yellow teeth struggled to break the skin. He chewed slowly, glancing at me.

I could feel his shame.

I opened my flask and poured some chamomile tea, sweetened with honey. His nostrils widened and after a sip I offered the cup. He drank, flinching from the heat, his lips twisting a growl, his eyes flashing with a glimpse of old power. I smiled and shrugged. "It's hot, be careful." He offered it to me, his face a grimace. I blew on the liquid and gave it back. He continued to drink and soon his expression relaxed.

"Why do you come?" His voice was like the whispering of leaves, the rumble of thunder, the burble of brooks and the pattering of rain on the forest floor. Again I shrugged, then looking around me at the wonder of nature and at a loss for words, I indicated the little wood and the view saying, "Because it's beautiful and helps me feel alive."

"Then why am I dying?" His voice cracked as he handed me the cup. I didn't know what to say. How could I apologise for the human race, when I knew they would not stop until everything was dead. Sighing, I replaced the cup and flask into my rucksack and watched the boughs of the hazel sway and dance in the breeze. A squirrel screeched from above and I noticed a black-nosed prickly rustling under a pile of leaves, uncurling from hibernation.

"Walk with me?" I asked, and he nodded. At first he struggled to stand, his crumpled limbs buckled under a body so frail that he fell to the mud. I thought he'd disappeared, but a gnarled hand reached out and I helped him, taking his weight whilst he slipped and tottered on shaky bent legs, to stand on crumbling hooves, quivering.

We moved slowly to the edge of the grove and listened to the tapping drum of a woodpecker shaping a nest deep in the bowels of a tree. Honeysuckle had begun to tangle itself through the shrubs, twisting and turning, the small clusters of green not yet ready for blooming the heady sweet fragrance that would engulf this side of the wood in summer. As I breathed the sharp fresh scent of spring he did too. His aged nut-brown nostrils cracked and flared, his eyes opened wider to absorb the scene of green life emerging, the cold earth birthing once more.

My eyes closed and I heard his breath snort forth, and my mind's eye saw the proud king strut and cajole with the woodland creatures leaping over the mountains, a haunting tune in his wake. He was tall and muscled, toned and handsome, his skin smooth to the touch, covered with downy hair that smelt of animal musk, both raw and primal. My vision joined his and I gasped at the wild and vigorous land stretching before me through eyelids held shut.

That ancient view was not divided into patchwork farms; rather, the swaying heads of trees swarmed up the sides of mountains giving way only to the golden gorse or purple heather shrubs that crowned the crags. Even the sea shone with crystal intensity, the power station just a future nightmare, unformed. I gripped his hand and opened my eyes when, weakly, he sagged against me. Taking the brittle body into my arms I carried him back to the hazel grove and placed his twisted form safely in the hollow of a tree.

Tears were flowing down my cheeks and I wiped them away, not wanting him to feel my pity. What worth is the pity of a silly weeping woman to his kind? He began to whimper once more and his breath slowed. I kissed his scarred and scabbed cheeks, my lips catching against the coarseness of his skin. His little hoof slipped out of the hollow and I repositioned him, tucking him in safely and womb-like out of sight.

"They are coming," he said. "Even now I can feel the earth tremble beneath the huge machines that tear and murder." I lowered my eyes, not wanting to know, but I knew he was right.

"I can still see you, and have done for years," I stated, attempting to sound positive, like a mother consoling a child with lies. A low wheezy rumble escaped his lips and I thought he was choking so I helped him sit up, then realised it was a chuckle. He held my face in his small twiggy hands, sharp and bark-like on my cheeks. His eyes bored into mine, beady like a blackbird's.

"That's because you believe," he said simply, and his chapped lips, edged with sap-like spittle, brushed my forehead in a woody kiss. Tears blurred my sight causing me to blink and I inhaled the scent of decaying wood. My eyes refocused and where a knotted brown hand had gripped my own, a hazel branch, green with buds, pressed into my palm. I traced my fingers over the rough-shaped knoll of the tree where his outline remained carved in bark.

I planted the branch in my garden and watched it take root and thrive, becoming a sapling and then a small tree. I celebrated when the first male catkins sprouted in winter and relished in gathering the abundance of hazelnuts for Yule. The old hazel wood and most of the fields are long gone these days. A housing estate has grown in their place and litter decorates the land like cancerous moles.

I never saw the sad beast again but every midsummer I hear an uncanny fluting and imagine I see him curve his body forth from the young hazel in my garden and spring leaping and cavorting through the land. He is followed by an array of forgotten creatures streaming forth on hoof, wing and claw.

I lean out of my bedroom window into the cool evening air and relish the sensation of goose-bumps pricking my skin through the thin silk of my blouse. "I believe I believe I believe," I cry out, watching June's rose-blushed moon rise over the rooftops. The scent of musk hangs heavy in the night and the soft brush of beasty breath dances along my spine to tremble through my hair, and my heart flutters to the beat of a cloven hoof.

Author note: When I wrote 'The Fall of Pan,' I wanted to raise awareness about our changing environment and how the pagan ways of worshipping nature and the land have been forgotten. I thought about the wildlife and how these majestic beasts lose their strength as they become elderly, an old fox, mangy and tired, scrounging in city bins or a stag scared and scabbed with past wounds, his antlers broken and I wondered what of the strutting god Pan? How would he look as a dying deity? Would he cease to exist because we simply don't believe anymore and what of the land? Will it die too, if we no longer believe in the old ways? This is one of my favourite stories and was first published with Black Shuck Books in a fantastic anthology entitled *Dreamland: Other stories* edited by the wonderful Sophie Essex.

# Jack and the Juniper Tree

*Eyes stare sharp with authority, fingers tap, impatient. Accusing glances flick with muttering spitting accusations. Whispers rustle, heads nod. Murderer…guilty…cold bitch … evil witch.*

I am condemned before I've even told my tale, but tell it I will.

Once upon a time …

In a land of blood and bone, my belly swollen with child, I staggered through the forest. He would be home today and I had to get rid of this thing. The dates did not match. He had been gone for over a year and this morning a letter had arrived, saying he had docked at the port, and I was to expect him for dinner. I had no meat and no way of buying any. This cumbersome beast in my womb had destroyed my figure and any man that passed my cottage refused my charms, leaving me penniless.

It had been my own fault. I had been careless; damn that old goat that had left his spawn inside me. I had bled as normal so not noticed the life quickening until it had begun to wriggle. The herbs I'd mixed had not helped get rid, but this brisk walk and the tea I'd overdosed on should hurry the birth along. It should be out before tonight.

The contractions began slow and irregular, and then more frequent. I had done this before but never birthed a living soul. They had all been cold and grey in death. I collapsed and landed heavily. It was about to begin, so I lay back against the rough bark of a juniper tree. I could smell the sharp pungent berries warmed by the late autumn sun. The moss was soft and I began to drift in and out of consciousness, as the pains rose and fell like the sea, and waited.

Agony tore through my womb and I screamed and scrambled, heedless of being heard. I was deep enough in the forest for my cries to not be noticed by any but old spirits and the dead. On hands and knees I felt the creature free itself from the confines of my body and fall to the leafy floor. Then a sound, soft to begin with, then crying with such force and strength enough to fill the silence, and I realised I had birthed a living child.

I picked up the tiny scrap and placed it to my breast. Eyes blinked with life, lips nuzzled and much to my astonishment it suckled greedily. I had never felt the breath of a child that lived before. Tears flowed down my cheeks to dampen the soft fuzzy head, and for a time I forgot my troubles and did nothing but lie in the late afternoon sunlight breathing the scent of juniper, whilst suckling my new baby boy.

I felt the afterbirth pass and suddenly I was afraid. I would have to go home and make food for my husband. He would wonder where I was and would beat me if I had no dinner for him. I looked longingly at my baby. I could never take him home; my husband would think nothing of sticking him with his sword and roasting him on a spit. 'I will leave you to the mercy of this kind juniper tree and return in the night to feed you again,' I assured him, cooing until he settled.

I had no plan as I had believed the baby would be born dead like all the others, and then I could have cooked him up and fed him to my husband, but he was alive and well. I gathered soft moss and crackling dead leaves. Under the tree was a hollow nestled in the roots. I made a little bed and lay my baby down, marvelling at his blood-red puckered lips and snow-white skin. He gurgled as I kissed him.

The afterbirth lay dark and slimy amongst the roots, its smell acrid and pungent. I gathered it in my shawl and carried it home for my husband's dinner. I rinsed it in the stream and placed it in a pan over the fire and added some beets. It was thick and rich with blood; surely he would be pleased. I had just enough time to wash myself and put on my best dress before I heard him arrive.

The ground shook and the crockery rattled as his huge form came up the path. I had forgotten just how large my husband was and fear burned within my belly. The door swung inwards and his great head appeared.

'Wife!' he bellowed. 'Where are you?'

'I am here,' I replied meekly, keeping my eyes downcast.

He gathered me in his arms and kissed me. I tried not to

show my revulsion as I gagged at his sour breath and struggled in his grasp. I was lucky he was hungry and quickly dished out the stew made of afterbirth. I consumed only the broth to replenish my strength. Noticing he had a large flagon of wine, I slyly added some poppy to ensure he slept after his food. I could have done with the pain easing properties myself, but knew I had to get back to the juniper tree to feed my baby.

As my husband slumbered, sated and fat, I thought about killing him. Bashing his skull or slitting his throat would be easy would it not? But how would I explain this to his friends and the villagers, who would, no doubt, ask questions. I would never be able to dispose of his body without help and murder was punishable by death. I'd have to be far away before his body was discovered and maybe they'd come after me, hunt me down for the spectacle of an execution. With these thoughts in mind I grabbed my shawl to return to my babe in the woods.

The juniper tree gleamed silver with starlight as I approached but I couldn't hear my baby. I hoped he was still asleep. Worrying, and praying no predators had come, drawn by the birthing smells, cautiously I pulled the branches and leaves aside, cooing softly, to reveal an empty nest. With a cry I pressed my face into the hollow of the tree shoving the moss aside and saw a dark tunnel reaching down to a great distance, where daylight glimmered. Pushing my head and shoulders into the passage I dragged my body inside and struggled towards the light.

Falling from the darkness I found myself clinging to the stalk of a huge plant that branched and joined with the roots of the juniper tree. Of my own land I could see nothing, only mist and fog swirling otherworldly in the silence. Hurriedly, and now terrified for my baby, I began to climb down. Passing large pods of dangling green beans, I realised it was a beanstalk to which I clung. Soon the fog began to lift, dispersing into marbled swirls, and the soft tones of a woman singing fluttered on the breeze.

The ground was close, only a few spirals of fog remaining, as I jumped the rest of the way and landed with a gasp. The woman immediately stopped singing and I heard a baby cry. Running towards it I reached out my arms through the clearing mist, and saw a tiny, red-caped old woman rocking my baby. She clutched him tight with sinewy arms, her white hair wisping over his face. Eyes widened in shock as she took in my presence. Stepping slowly backwards, squaring crooked shoulders, she demanded my name and told me nobody but her son Jack had ever climbed the beanstalk before: only he had the right.

I began to weep and explained where I had come from and what had happened, assuring her she had nothing to fear. She handed me my baby and he quietened once I placed him to my breast. I noticed she lived on what looked like a prosperous farm surrounded by forest on all sides. There was a track winding through the trees and it was from there I heard the beat of hooves. A horse and cart emerged with a young man at the reins; the back was laden with goods.

The old woman's son was handsome but small like his mother, and his eyes flashed when he saw me, making me blush. Coyly, I looked away.

'What brings such a pretty young woman, nursing a babe, out here to our farm?' he enquired of his mother whilst holding my eye.

'She came down the beanstalk after her baby.'

'The beanstalk, eh?' he said, eyeing it and me curiously. 'Only I am allowed to ascend the beanstalk, so tell me how you descended. Do you come from above?'

'Yes, I do,' I said and told my story for the second time that day.

'Then please stay with us for dinner, we have plenty of meat. Surely you do not need to go home yet?' I was frightened, but even more frightened of returning home to my husband and my hunger had the better of me.

During dinner, Jack and his mother assured me that my baby could stay with them and I could visit whenever I wanted. Even stay for good, if that was my wish. Of course I wished to get away from my husband but there was something odd about this mother and son living alone in this strange land. Whatever I decided, I had to get back to my house, where my husband would no doubt have gold and silver from his recent return. I needed to steal enough so I could start a new life with my child.

Jack and his mother promised to look after my baby whilst I returned to my husband. I assured them I would not be long and would pay them for their trouble. They laughed and nodded as they waved me off. Jack had wanted to come with me to help, he was confident he did not fear my husband, but I knew my husband's temper. His sheer size dwarfed both Jack and his mother. Even I was large in comparison to them. So I told him to leave it to me, plus I had an uncanny feeling that Jack may want to steal some of my husband's money for himself and might possibly scupper my chance of escape.

I returned to the beanstalk, to the juniper tree and to my house tucked deep in the woods. Luckily my husband was still asleep; the poppy had worked well. I gathered a few of my clothes, wrapped up in a shawl, and approached my husband's purse. He had been successful during his trip. It bulged with gold and silver. Slowly I edged it open and took some of the shining coins.

'What are you doing, thief?' came his booming voice.

'I am only counting how much money your glorious self has made, my love.' I realised then that I would have to kill him if I was ever to leave with anything that night and I could not bear to be separated from my baby any longer. I wasn't sure if leaving him with Jack and his mother had been a wise decision and I was eager to return.

'Here, have some more wine and we can celebrate your hard work and fortune,' I said filling his glass with the poppy-laced wine. He raised it in my direction and downed it in one. I stoked up the fire knowing that the heat would help him sleep and waited. Soon he was snoring once again, and I crept to the kitchen returning with the knife I used for cutting and gathering my roots and plants. I kept it very sharp.

I watched my husband slumber. I had been his since my monthly blood began. The night he came to fetch me from my father's cabin lay etched upon my mind, my father cowering as he handed me and my small dowry over to the beast. I had no mother to cling to, as I had killed her tearing myself forth from the womb. I hoped my husband would be loving and tender, but he knew nothing of these ways. Killing him was something I'd dreamed of, but until now had never had the courage. Women were burned on pyres for the simple kindness of healing the sick... In truth, men feared us and, as my husband stirred, I wondered if they had just cause.

My thoughts were often evil and more than once I had been tempted to use witchcraft to raise a storm and sink his ship. There had been talk in the village of the small people again, the thieves that crept and stole in the night; I hoped he would be accosted in the forest and murdered for his precious items, but fortune was not my ally as he continued to darken my door, but at least he brought coin. Should I not be thankful, I wondered? I suppose I had been, but not anymore. Now I had a reason to fight, a reason to kill and be free, and a reason to live for the sake of my child – a reason to commit murder.

Holding the little knife tightly, in palms salty with sweat, I wondered how I should do it, how I could end his life fast without the risk of him waking and killing me instead. My hands trembled and I thought of how the pigs were slaughtered; slice to the neck and his life blood would flow. Except that took time and my husband's neck was heavy with jowls -what if I missed the vital artery? Or failed to sever it all the way, meaning he would survive, fight back? I knew I had one attempt to kill or be killed.

My knife was too small to reach down to his heart, so it would have to be the jugular. His heavy boots were propped upon a stool and he had loosened the leather thongs that bound them. I tied the strips together tightly; if he tried to chase after me, he would fall, allowing me to complete my crime. I toyed with tying his huge hands too, but feared he would wake. I had to act now if I was going to act at all. Breathing deeply, I raised the knife, watching closely for the small thrum in his fat neck, and stabbed him deep in his throat.

He woke and roared, clutching the wound but I acted fast and quickly ripped the knife to the side pulling it out. The knife slipped from my grip as the blood sprayed forth, drenching me. His eyes registered what I had done, shock flickering as his pupils faded. Lunging towards me, he staggered – the tied leather boots tripping him – and he toppled over; a mighty oak felled. I sprang away and just managed to avoid him before he landed, tipping the flagon and hitting his head on the hearthstone. A dark stain spread outwards to mingle with the spilt wine.

Trembling with fear and adrenalin I ran to the river, where I washed the blood from my body and hair. The water swirled berry red in the moonlight and I shivered. My breasts were heavy with milk and painful to touch. I must have looked a terrifying sight, a wicked witch who had murdered her husband in cold blood. I returned to the house, strangely nervous at the dead thing that had caused me so much pain. I crept forward and with shaking hands checked for a pulse of life. There was none, his hulk was nothing but flesh, bone and blood. I dressed hurriedly in warm clothes, I needed to be gone. I didn't want any of his friends calling round to welcome his return and accuse me of murder.

Quickly I ran to the purse of coins and took the lot. Now, if I was ever discovered I could claim I had been kidnapped by the robbers who had killed my husband. I knew his friends would search for me and I'd have to get to the strange land fast. I couldn't leave anything to chance, I had a babe to think of now. As I reached the juniper tree, I noticed a striking bird with red and white plumage alight on the lowest branch. It looked at me knowingly then began to sing a beautiful song, but the words that formed in the tuneful trills chilled me:

My Mother she birthed me

My Father would eat me

The others they ate me

And my bones lie under the beanstalk

'What is this horror…?' I cried, and shooing the bird away I descended the beanstalk. It was still dark in the land below but I noticed freshly dug earth at the bottom. I scraped back the soil with my hands and there, wrapped neatly in a silk cloth, were what appeared to be the bones of my baby, freshly picked clean of sweet pink flesh. I ran my fingers over the glistening remains and wept, cradling them to my heart. I hadn't even named him.

Seeking revenge I entered Jack's cottage. Loud, even, sleeping breaths slumbered through the hall and a rich, sickly scent of meat lingered in the air. The first door I opened held a comfortable cot bed pushed up against the wall. I approached to see the old lady sleeping deeply. I picked up a soft white pillow. Her eyes snapped open and I relished the fear that flickered behind her rheumy gaze before I smothered her. The small body bucked and kicked as I pressed until her foul life fled. She was an easy kill, but Jack would be harder.

In the kitchen I found a cleaver. I touched the soft silk cloth that held my baby's bones, which I had placed in my pocket, and fuelled by anger I sneaked into Jack's room. A golden egg sat at the side of an empty bed. I remembered a villager complaining of his golden goose being stolen, and it seemed I had found the culprit. It seemed these two must be the same as those stealthy small people I had heard of, who came thieving and killing in the night. Jack was awake and he slammed the bedroom door, trapping me. Smirking, he raised a sharp pointed blade.

I raised the cleaver and lunged towards him, hoping to cut him in two, but although I was the larger, he was a skilled fighter and I was weak. He side-stepped me. My cleaver caught in the door and I felt a sharp stab in my side; kicking out I knocked Jack to the floor, where he twisted to his feet once more and grinned. I knew when I was out of my depth, and tugged to release the cleaver, swinging the door inwards, and ran, toppling cupboards and shelves in my wake in a bid to slow his pursuit. I reached the beanstalk and threw myself into its boughs still holding the cleaver, and climbed as fast as I could. My side pained where I had been stabbed but it was nothing to the hurt I had already endured.

Jack followed swiftly and I could feel him gaining on me. On reaching the juniper tree, I pushed myself through the opening and breathless turned back to hang from the roots. They curled and held me firm, recognising my need, and with all my might I hacked at the top of the beanstalk where it branched into several tendrils that clung to the roots. Thankfully, the cleaver was still sharp and as Jack's head emerged his eyes locked onto mine and I heard the last tendrils of the beanstalk breakaway from the branch he had ascended. The stalk swayed but Jack hung on and reached for another branch, his eyes full of rage.

I hacked at the next, breaking the sinews, but Jack had reached the juniper's roots. I had the advantage and, caring little for my own safety, in my grief hurled myself forwards swinging the cleaver, slicing Jack's head clean from his body. I watched his head and corpse plummet down through the swirling mist and fog into the silence below. The beanstalk quivered before all the remaining tendrils unfurled to twist and disentangle from the roots of the tree and slowly it, too, began to fall, joining Jack on his descent.

Heaving my body upwards, I collapsed in the hollow where I had birthed my only living child and wept. My tears soaked into the silk that held my baby's bones and I buried them under the tree, marking the spot with a stone. As I wept and mourned for my son, the pretty little bird returned and sat upon my shoulder and sang. The mournful tweets swirled into words as they touched and prodded my mind.

My Mother she loved me

The wicked Jack ate me

My Mother she avenged me

'Oh shush, shush!' I yelled at the bird, pressing my palms to my ears, not wanting to be reminded of what had befallen my child, but it ignored me and pecked at the stone under which I had buried my babe.

The ground began to move, the fallen leaves swirled and I heard a muffled cry. I pushed the stone aside and a small white finger reached through the disturbed earth. I scraped at the soil and there in the cloth, instead of bones, lay my boy, snuggled in a leafy bower. He gurgled and hiccupped before continuing to cry. I delighted at the sound and held him before me, checking he was complete before holding him at my breast. He latched on and greedily began to feed before snuggling to sleep. 'Thank you!' I cried to the little bird, which bobbed upon the branches of the juniper before disappearing into the air. A soft red and white feather fell to my lap and I tucked it into my shawl.

Exhausted, I lay against the juniper tree and breathed deep the sweet milky scent of my baby mingling with the woody spice of the berries warmed by the sun. I knew I couldn't go home, and the beanstalk was gone, so I would have to hide in the forest like a cut-throat – after all, that is what I'd become. I had killed three people and one of them my own husband.

Murderer, said the voices; murderer murderer murderer, echoed the muttering; guilty guilty guilty, rustled the condemning whispers in my mind.

'Yes, I am,' I announced. 'My husband's death could never be blamed on the little people or a mere woman, oh no I must be a witch most evil to have killed such a mighty figure – and someday I'll pay for my crimes. If those pompous old men in the courts don't burn me, then the lifeless God will dish out his penance no doubt ... but not yet. For now, I am a mother.' I tasted the word on my lips, breathed the word on my breath, watched it form and felt its power.

'Mother...' I whispered and laughed. 'I am a mother above all else and I would kill again to save my son ... so judge me if you dare.' My babe stirred within my shawl, the red and white feather brushed his delicate skin and he began to suckle.

Author note: 'Jack and the Juniper Tree' was written for a submission call for a Welsh women write crime anthology entitled *Cast a long Shadow* by Honno Press. Crime is not my genre, but I wanted to contribute so much to this important call. Thinking about it I realised that fairytales are full of crime: murder, cannibalism, theft and abuse. So, I decided to choose two tales, 'Jack and the Beanstalk' and 'The Juniper Tree' and do the popular mashing of both together. I then wrote from the perspective of the giant's wife highlighting domestic abuse, the importance of motherhood and the plight of women throughout the ages, and of course the accusatory label of 'witch' rendering them powerless to be believed regardless of their actions.

# The Sleeping Giant

My Gran often spoke of the sleeping giant on a hill in the valleys of South Wales. He'd swallow a child if they were not careful, she'd say, reminding me of a boy who got lost and was never found again. Only his trainer was left, complete with foot, resting against the craggy lip of the giant. The local villagers avoided walking across him for fear of his waking. My parents moved away when I was fourteen so apart from a mind's eye vision of the huge man stretched out above the road, I'd not seen him for about ten years.

Since then, the area has become littered with tourists and walkers oblivious to the fact he might just wake up and swallow one of them if they happened to be stomping across his face. I'd told my girlfriend Mia about the area, and she'd heard how beautiful the countryside was and seemed eager to visit. So begrudgingly I decided to take her there for a holiday.

My gran had long since passed and my parents had sold her cottage which was now a holiday let. A tiny abode but renovated to a good standard, and nothing like how I remembered. I felt like a stranger here these days.

"Pull over," cried Mia as the giant's sleeping form came into view on the approach road. "I want to get a photo of this." I pulled into a lay-by, and we got out of the car.

"Has he really swallowed people?"

"Apparently he's had loads," I said. Mia laughed, taking a selfie with the giant in the background.

"He looks a bit like you," she said, as we got back into the car. People used to say the same about my granddad, but I didn't tell her that.

The cottage sat low in the opposite valley. There was a patio outside where my gran would have sat on her old wooden chair, next to the bright mix of coloured hollyhocks, cleaning green beans or popping peas. She said she could keep an eye on him from there and make sure he didn't wake up without her knowing. I used to wonder what she would do if he ever did wake up. How did knowing about it help? She'd still be trampled or eaten either way. I'd rather not know, not witness him rise from his stony bed.

The hollyhocks were dead now, just keeling over seed pods, and with a modern click the front door opened. The wooden table where gran prepared cawl against a stove-blackened brick chimney had given way to a contemporary stylish kitchen. The old flagstone floor, where a pile of furred moggies heaped in front of the fire, remained but was glazed and lacquered to match the marble tops. The moggies were long gone, but probably still mithering gran for scraps.

"Very nice," said Mia. "Your parents were mad to sell this place."

"It didn't look like this then."

That evening we ate out at the local pub. There were a few tourist types hanging around with kids, but the bar was mainly propped up by locals. The menu was basic, so we opted for burger and chips to go with the fine ale on offer.

"Don't get too drunk," giggled Mia. "I'll never remember the footpath home."

"I'll be fine, don't want you being a tasty treat for the big man on the hill."

"Oh, don't freak me out, but I'm definitely up for a walk there tomorrow. I dare you to sit on his nose."

"I dare you to stand on his mouth," I countered watching her face squirm as she seriously thought about it.

"When was the last time he ate someone?"

I glanced at the missing persons pictures dotting the notice board of the pub. "Ten years ago by the looks of it."

She leant across me to see the last mugshot staring out from a cluster of others.

"He was only a kid," she said her voice losing its earlier mirth.

The boy's face was familiar; maybe we'd gone to the same school.

"Aye, the giant don't care," said the bartender. "He was a bright lad too, but not bright enough. Should have stayed away." He wiped a glass and replaced it before saying, "Where you from then?"

"Jack's local," said Mia before I could think whether I wanted my presence known or not. The barman squinted at me.

"Well bugger me, it's not young Jack Stone? Grandson to old Nan Stone?"

"Yep, that's me."

"Well, well, welcome back stranger, and this is your…" he glanced at Mia.

"I'm Mia, his girlfriend and I've come to slay the giant." She held out her hand and the old barman took it and laughed. A few locals looked up from their pints and joined in like jackdaws.

"Well, fancy that," was all he said as he shuffled off to change a barrel.

"Slay the giant?" I raised an eyebrow.

"Maybe not," she shrugged.

The walk back to the house in the dark was fun, but Mia was noisy, whooping and singing. I prayed she wouldn't wake him, as I'd drunk a few too many and didn't feel capable of slaying a fly let alone a giant.

Thankfully we'd left the outside light on and before long the little cottage loomed into view. Inside was warm and cosy and soon I forgot about it being gran's old house as Mia stripped off and we fell into bed.

Spent, and wrapped around Mia's soft body, I had no trouble falling asleep but woke with an alcohol induced thirst and headache. Creeping downstairs, I poured a glass of water from the kitchen tap and took two paracetamols. I stepped outside into the cool air and sat on the bench. A tawny owl was yipping in the old oak; it sounded like a youngster. There was a slight smell in the air of rock and earth which reminded me of grandad, and I tried not to think about him… didn't want his memory to stir and awaken things in my own.

Grandad had worked at the quarry. Left before daybreak and came home after sundown. Nan liked it that way, she preferred him not being around. There was a place called Penwyllt which in Welsh translates to wild head. Ah God, didn't I have some wild times up there as a teen. There were caves, the whole hill was riddled with them, some man made, but others old and natural, part of the land. None of us lads were brave enough to go down them though. We just got pissed and lit fires in the old quarry pits and smoked weed when we could get it.

Some said the quarry was another giant, but he'd been killed by us lot, well, mankind I suppose, many years ago, and we'd quarried inside his head making him wild and crazy, hence the name. Anyway, those tunnels are like being inside him, walking along the nerve pathways of his brain. I hated the caves. Grandad took me there once – the old bastard knew I was afraid; did it deliberate, he was like that.

The entrance to the oldest part was under what looked like a huge eyebrow; heavy and thick it was and covered in that bushy lichen stuff they go on about in nature programmes. It was like walking into his head through his eye. Fool's gold glistened on the walls and an odd white fungus grew there. The walls ran red though – iron is what Grandad called it, said the old bugger had lots of iron in his blood.

He spent lots of time up those caves and quarries did Grandad, learning that old giant's thoughts. I've never been back inside that old head. Too scared I'll start thinking the same things and that wouldn't be good – maybe that's what happened to Grandad. I didn't tell Mia about those caves either, she'd just want to explore, and I don't think I could do that again. Just being here was enough.

The bench shook a bit then, like your bed does when someone treads on the floorboards waking you up, but you don't want to wake because you think there's someone there. I remembered keeping my eyes squeezed shut when that happened. Trying not to see the shadow, the outline of something, but the smell gave it away. The stench of hewn rock and blasting powder and the sulphuric bowels of the earth blown open and Grandad saying they were mining the very arse of the old sod on the hill.

I wondered how the other giant felt, just lying there sleeping whilst we crawled all over his mate, carving him open like a carcass at the butcher's. Parts of him trundling along the old

Brecon railway line to be used for building houses and whatnot. We never used them stones for the village; the village was here long before. The stones from that Wild Head Quarry built the local towns, cursing them with poverty, drug abuse and things that happen behind closed doors. An apt revenge.

The sky was a swirl of planets and galaxies and the hill where the lonely giant slept lay flat and empty. My eyes scanned the darkness until I could make out his form, much closer now, forming a large irregular hill. He sat there and saluted me, his outline just like Grandad when he sat on my bed. He would salute in just the same way. My body trembled with the bench as memories rubbed and poked. I closed the door on the night, not wanting to see more and crept upstairs to bed. Mia stirred, and I shushed her, relieved she didn't wake.

I dreamt my gran was calling me for breakfast and I went down the old rickety staircase wearing my blue flannelette pyjamas I had as a boy. I noticed my feet were dirty like I'd been outside barefoot or something.

"Nice of you to come and see me Jack," she said. "I hoped you wouldn't but then you never listened. Your parents took you away to avoid this from happening, but it's done now, you can't change the past."

"What do you mean?" I said, tucking into toast with butter and honey and trying to hide my feet when I saw her tut and shake her head.

"You'll see."

"Jack, wake up." It was Mia. "I've been waiting for ages. Let's get out for a walk and have breakfast later."

"At least let me have a coffee, I feel like I've been awake all night." I moaned as she handed me a steaming mug. I sipped the restorative liquid whilst starring at my filthy feet. I must have gone outside barefoot again. Gran would have clobbered me for dirtying the sheets.

Before long I was traipsing after Mia along the giant's chest. I should have known when I saw the mugshot of that boy the previous night. It was all coming back to me now, my family's past and why the other kids stopped wanting to be around me.

As we reached his face Mia skirted his cheeks. "Go on, dare

me to stand on his mouth."

"Okay," I said. "I dare you to stand on his mouth."

"Sit on his nose then," she said.

I stepped over an eye making sure it was closed and stumbling slightly clambered onto his nose to sit on the pocked rocky tip.

She edged forward circling his chin before scrambling onto his lips and stood there looking past me and into his stony gaze.

"Come on you old bastard, eat me then," she yelled.

A red kite keened overhead searching for carrion, swooping like an angel robed in russet towards the giant's hands as two crows followed.

"Come on," I said getting up. "Let's have breakfast at the pub."

On the way down we could see a few cars parked in the pub car park including a police car.

"Bloody hell," said Mia, "I wonder what's happened.

"We'll soon find out," I said, although I had a bad feeling.

Sombre faces greeted us, and the barman gave me a nod. A child had gone missing, snatched from his bed in the night, the window broken.

I joined in the search party to scour the mountain paths, but once again the giant was blamed. Hair and scalp were found on his fingers as if he'd tugged the strands from his mouth before swallowing. I remembered his mocking salute the night before, just like my grandfather sitting on the edge of my bed in the dark.

Mia and I returned to London that night vowing never to come back, but as the years slip by, I know I will. The giant lives on inside us Stones; I'll never be a stranger no matter how hard I try. It's our family legacy, the pain, and the shame. It'll never leave us. It's all part of the landscape, part of the land, just like the giant. Ingrained too deeply to ever forget.

Author note: 'The Sleeping Giant' is a story I thought up whilst walking upon and around the very real sleeping giant, also known as *Cribarth* in Welsh, and the area of Penwyllt in the valleys of South Wales. I frightened myself thinking of *him* waking and there being nothing left of me but maybe my foot complete with boot, or my hair. The story takes on a darker side when I thought about sinister things that go on behind closed doors and how they get covered up, ignored, emerging in folktales or ghost stories. Writing in a somewhat magical realism style the story never really reveals if the giant is real or if it's the Stone family that are responsible. The grandfather, sitting on the bed of young Jack saluting just like the giant, and should young Jack Stone have stayed away like his grandmother told him in his dream? This story came second in the 2022 Hay writers' circle, Frances Copping memorial prize.

# The Cloying Scent of Apples

It has been twelve days since the car accident that stole my parents, what is left of them will be buried tomorrow, day thirteen of all days. I try not to be superstitious but can't always help it. People have been kind; they know I'm a strange breed. I mean I fear everything, but the thing that frightens me most is the fear itself, and the irrational madness that surges through my mind as a result. I was a nervous child my mother used to say, and later an introverted teenager.

I was bright at school but didn't do well in my exams because I was afraid. Everybody fears exams but my fear was heightened to almost blind panic. Quite what I was afraid of I don't really know. I just remember going to bed with my stomach a knot of anxiety dreading the morning – and the night too. The darkness crept along the landing and in through my door, edging across the floor to nudge against my bed. I had a tiny night light in the shape of a mushroom, and it was this and sometimes the moon that kept the darkness at bay.

Not that the moon was always a comfort, playing peek a boo from behind a cloud. She'd reach into my soul to illuminate my weakness, but I feared the darkness even more. The glowing mushroom was a weak and insufficient substitute, but at least it stopped the dark reaching my pillow. I remember that the mushroom had a small creature sitting beside it: why do people believe children love fairies and mushrooms? They're not called fey for nothing. So, the tiny comfort I had was scuppered by that wicked face peering at me from beneath the glowing gills of a mad fungus…

We lived on the coast. An idyllic spot, though I trembled if there was a storm. The thought of being washed out of my bed and into the cold deep was too much to bear and I would scream all night. My mother held me safe as Father looked on, concern creasing his brows. Later that concern became anger and frustration, but he tried not to show it, although I could feel his disappointment and embarrassment at having such a cowardly son.

As other kids took to surfing and hanging out on the beach, I huddled indoors, too afraid of the sea and what lay in her depths to accompany them. As I got older, I would take a heavy dose of sleeping pills if there was a storm forecast or even high winds. The double glazing helped.

Mother's favourite place was under the apple tree in the garden. She would sit there on a recliner for hours reading, while I played on a blanket at her feet glancing nervously up at the tree. Its many knotted faces stared back. An apple dropped once, actually hitting me on the head, and leaving a drool of mush in my hair. I jumped up frantic, terrified that a worm or some other creepy crawler had escaped the pulp and wriggled into my scalp. Mother laughed, wiping my hair with a handkerchief and comforting me. She told me it brought wisdom just like Sir Isaac Newton, but I knew it was one of the devilish folk that adorned the branches.

Sometimes I heard voices all muttering at once, the smell of apples sickly and sweet, and I'd glimpse a terrible emptiness opening between the leaves and boughs. A whirlpool sensation would cause my head to spin, and giddy and weightless I'd feel myself being sucked into the void. A feeling not unlike I get when staring into the sea. Then I'd grip hold of mother's leg until the dizziness passed, and my heart rate steadied, and I'd be left with the nauseating scent of apples.

There was an old wooden plaque hanging in the tree, engraved with some kind of prayer or good luck wish. Father had brought it back from a visit to Japan when I was a child. It was just a piece of tourist rubbish, and I remember asking my parents what it meant. Behind false smiles they would fob me off with some good health, wealth and happiness nonsense. I didn't trust the thing and doubted my parents knew what the scribbled prayer really meant. They used to argue a lot back then. Something to do with another woman, and I wondered what would happen to me. Would this other woman be my stepmother? And how wicked would she be?

As an adult, I couldn't make the strange writing out either; even with the help of the internet for translation, I failed. The symbols had faded, from it having been left outside, but that is where they are supposed to hang, father would say. They are hung in outdoor shrines all over Japan as offerings to the spirits. I should remove it and burn it in the log burner, but I'm too afraid to touch it.

I was terrified of closing my curtains at night, because my room looked out at the apple tree. Mother used to draw them, so I didn't have to see its twisted faces leering at me before bed. One time Father made me do it myself, telling me to be brave, saying the monster was in my head and not real at all. I wanted to please him so much that I stood tall in front of the window and opened my eyes. I saw only my own reflection but there was something behind me, a black knotted shadow that I knew came from the tree, a thing from the void. I'd screamed and my father slapped me, his face sneering into disgust when he realised I'd wet myself.

Nevertheless, as a young man I learnt to manage the irrational part of myself. I took pills prescribed by the doctor, antipsychotic and anti-anxiety, which helped eventually. At first, I was frightened of the way my heart slowed, and a heavy fuzziness restricted my senses. I found that I couldn't react quickly enough which worried me because if I couldn't react when needed I'd not get away from whatever monstrosity I needed to get away from. This disorientation led back to a place of fear – fear of going insane. Soon however, my mind succumbed to the dissonance, and I became accustomed to the numbing effects of the drugs and realised it was preferable to the constant anxiety. Better to feel nothing than the fear.

My father had been a college lecturer and my mother a secretary. We were what people would call comfortably middle class. They sheltered me from the outside world, especially my mother, and with my father's help I managed to secure a job in accounting when I left college. It was a small local firm where I was alone most of the time in the office, happy to get on with it. It was a plain room with a small window and plastic blinds, which bizarrely helped me relax.

Mathematics had been the only thing to ease my fear in school. I mean, most kids hated it, but I'd discovered from an early age that repeatedly doing sums in my head and counting to ridiculously high numbers helped my thoughts to stabilize and banish any demons. Sitting in the quiet office working through spreadsheets and figures was the only place I found any kind of solace.

I had been given compassionate leave after my parent's accident but had returned to work pretty much straight after. I found the routine comforting – much better than going home. There I would be greeted by the noisy silence of an empty house, the grandfather clock clicking as the pendulum swung slowly back and forth, each prolonged second pushing my anxiety higher. Time slowed considerably and I began to count between the seconds, fumbling in my inside pocket where I kept my pills. The plastic strip crinkled reassuringly as I popped a couple out.

I was on a high dosage of various medications these days and had to be careful. The doctor wanted to see if they could be reduced, but it only resulted in fresh panic attacks whenever I tried. What was the lesser evil, the monster in my head or the drug? I swallowed the pills dry and took a deep steadying breath to stop the room from shaking – or was that me?

My head was beginning to sway as the drug took effect, and my racing heart eased its pace. The familiar marshmallow fug softened my senses, and I sat back onto the settee to wait for my parents to explain it had all been one big misunderstanding, and they were not dead. It was a state of mind I liked to trick myself into, a pretence that hoodwinked my thoughts into believing everything was as it was before. Sleep came to me easier that way.

A shrill ringing woke me with a start. My mouth was dry and slack, my tongue thick and I had crusted drool on my lips. My head swam with the usual dizziness that accompanied too many pills, but at least I was not panicking. The telephone shrieked again, and I staggered to my feet and managed to pick up the receiver.

"Hu, hu, hullo," I stammered as my mouth tried to form the greeting.

"Simon, its Henry, I'm just letting you know we'll be there in the morning to accompany you." I didn't reply.

"Simon? Are you okay?"

"Yes, I'm okay."

"Simon poor chap, don't worry about the funeral we'll be with you, in fact we can come over now if you'd like some company?"

"No, no…but thank you. I appreciate it but I'd rather be alone, I'm going to get an early night."

"Okay if you're sure, we'll leave you with your grief. Cecilia and I will see you tomorrow. Goodbye and try to get a good night's rest."

"Goodbye," I replied. I scanned the room for Grief. Was he here with me?

The absence of Henry's voice left a stale emptiness in the air, causing my heart to race and my mind to think irrationally. I was afraid of that monster called Grief. I didn't usually drink but Father always kept a fine quality whisky in the old teak cabinet, and I fumbled with the glasses, my hands weak and shaky. The smell of smoky peat and creosote wafted under my nose, and I poured a good two-inch measure. I didn't add any water, like Father did, but knocked it back straight.

My eyes closed and the whisky tumbler rolled across the hardwood floor before stopping abruptly. In my mind I tried to picture what it had stopped against. I was sure it had rolled in the direction of the chair next to the hearth, and if so, it would have continued to knock against the skirting boards.

Slowly I opened my eyes to look, half expecting to see Father sitting there with a whisky of his own. Instead, lounging in the ox-blood Queen Anne was a dirty despicable creature, the tumbler caught under its large, cracked leather boot. The figure lent forward to retrieve it and I staggered back in shock as a smile drew itself across a shadowed face. The rational part of my brain quickly informed me there was nobody there. How could there be? I turned and ran into the kitchen. It was the whisky and too many pills.

My stomach heaved and I retched up the peaty malt and a load of bile into the sink watching it splash onto the morning's dirty cereal bowl. With a sour taste in my mouth, I filled a glass of water and drank deeply. Looking at my reflection in the window I saw a haggard fearful person all alone in the world, with nobody to ease their fear, only grief. No sooner had I thought it than I heard a slow tread behind me, and a terrible face loomed up alongside my own.

Hollowed out eyes rheumy and yellowed looked at me, a large nose reddened by drink dominated sunken cheeks and a weak chin. Wiry lips parted to reveal a chipped and broken discoloured smile, or rather a hard done-by grimace. Sloping shoulders and a pigeon chest were draped in an old wax jacket, greasy and worn, hanging down to bony knees encased in stained denim, and ending in misshapen boots, scuffed and rotten.

"G – g – get out…get out of my house," I stammered desperately, searching in my jacket pocket for my mobile phone. It buzzed in my hand. Shocked I glanced at the screen. It was Jan, my social worker.

"Jan."

My voice was high pitched and erratic as my eyes scanned an empty kitchen.

"Simon, how are you?"

My voice stuck in my throat as I realised, I was alone.

"Simon, are you okay?"

"Err I'm fine Jan honestly," I replied, my voice settling into the lie.

"Are you sure? I can call round if you'd like a nice cuppa and a chat?" Her voice sounded concerned.

"No, please I just need to rest. I'm not going to do anything stupid, don't worry. I'm far too fearful for that nonsense."

"Okay, if you're sure but call me if you change your mind."

"Yes, of course. I'm… I'm having an early night."

"That sounds like a good idea. I'll be round in the morning to help with everything; you don't have to face this alone Simon."

"Thank you, Jan," I said hurriedly. "See you in the morning."

I hung up not waiting for her reply. I couldn't face seeing her tonight. I know she was only doing her job and checking to see if I was a danger to myself or others, but I didn't want another talking-to about reducing my medication. Sighing, I refilled my glass of water and had decided to go to bed when a sharp irregular knocking rapped at the back door making me jump.

I wished I hadn't been so quick to hang up on Jan as a steady *tap tap tap* followed, mocking the pounding of my heart as fear flared. I waited for it to stop, not sure if there was somebody there. Nobody would just turn up and knock on the back door surely? Then it came again, sharper this time, more urgent. I wondered if Jan had been outside and had detected the fear in my voice and decided to check up on me anyway.

"Who's there?" I found myself asking.

I was answered by another sharp knock. Cautiously I approached the door and opening it a crack peered into the remnants of a deep, lilac dusk. A twisted limb from the apple tree lay discarded against the door, thrown by the wind. I stole a glance at the lawn: more branches lay strewn claw-like amongst rotting apples. A sharp pungent smell, wild and earthy, wafted from the tree into my face. I picked up the branch and threw it at the tree, where the old Japanese plaque swivelled and danced. Shivering I closed the door, locking it firmly, and picking up my glass made my way upstairs.

I cursed myself for opening my bedroom curtains that morning, but with the light on I wouldn't be able to see the apple tree, only my own wretched reflection. I wasn't sure which I feared most. Carefully I placed the glass of water on my bedside cabinet and approached the window. My funeral suit hung ready where I had left it on the wardrobe door to air. Beyond it, the garden was lit by the living room lights I'd forgotten to put off, and there he was, sitting there just like Mother in her recliner under the twisted tree. He raised one hand and gave a plaintive wave, the Japanese plaque spinning in the wind above his head.

I knew what he was now: Grief. Whenever I thought of my parents he'd be there, there was no escape. In the distance the sea rolled, and I heard waves crashing against the shore. The night sky was heavy and restless. I'd learnt to live with Fear. I'd watched her contort the apple tree into sneering faces and poison the sea against me. But Grief – Grief was a different demon altogether. Angrily I drew the curtains and backed away from the window.

"No, no you don't," I shouted, "that's Mother's chair, get off it."

I ran downstairs shaking as I frantically unlocked the back door and stared at the empty recliner. The wind buffeted the tree shaking the branches with fury, mocking my bravado. I let out a shriek and slammed the door, locking it. A steady tapping started again as I backed out of the kitchen.

"Go away," I yelled, my voice belying my panic and I ran upstairs taking the steps two at a time.

Breathing hard I crawled into bed, pulled the covers over my head and wept. I'd taken too many pills; how foolish I'd been. A girlish chuckle accompanied my weeping as Fear joined my vigil, and the firm tread of Grief ascended the stairs. I held my breath, straining my ears. The steps paused, the door creaked, and the air filled with his foul rancid breath. Almost choking on my hiccupping sobs, I began to count backwards from twenty thousand clutching what little sanity I had left. But his cracked voice joined me in my sorrowful lament, until it was all I could hear.

The void began to open beyond the branches of the apple tree. Darkness expanded and reached into my room to pool onto the floor, and crawling forwards came the prayer from the Japanese plaque. Long inky tendrils spilled onto my pillow, and I felt cold fingers brush rotten apple pulp from my hair.

I shrank from the touch and felt myself falling into the cloying scent of apples, soft and sticky with rot. Desperately I tried to feel the firm bed beneath my body and the soft comfort of the duvet, but there was only damp decomposing earth where things wriggled and scuttled and gnawed. I must be outside and not in my bed at all. Had I fallen, I wondered, or had someone hit me with a branch from that wretched tree?

Biting and sucking strange inky symbols scraped and tore at my hair and scratched my face like bony fingers with tiny teeth and I gagged from the stench of decay. Blood rushed through my head roaring as Fear screamed her rotten laugh and far away, I thought I still heard a shaky voice counting steadily backwards as Grief's sneering tones mocked and reviled – just like Father. Weeping with shame I grovelled, and clasping my hands in front of my groin I frantically tried to hide the telltale spread of warmth.

Author note: I really felt sorry for Simon in 'The Cloying Scent of Apples'. He's neuro-diverse and not understood by his father, friends or teachers at the time of his growing up. There are hints of abuse issues, and he really is a fearful young man. Now he is on his own coming to terms with his grief and fear, and I just made his life even worse by giving them a physical presence. This interests me though, when emotions are so strong they are almost physical beings, never leaving you. Simon intrigued me too, as did the apple tree and the Japanese plaque, but it was Jan, his social worker who had a bigger story to tell. Her tale, complete with a journey to Japan has become a novel, which features Simon too, although Jan is the protagonist. Simon is happy to have a small part in the novel but prefers to remain in this story. He is okay after his ordeal, but fear and grief have never left his side.

# The Damson Tree

I saw the light take the others, but I held back. I felt life underground and followed that instead. I was only twelve when the fever took me. The damson tree they buried me under in the graveyard had been my favourite place. The headstone is a delightful pink marble. I can see it because I followed the slow drum of living tissue that collected water and nutrients from the earth. The same earth enclosing my body and the same nutrients my flesh expunged into the ground.

I can feel the tree's soul, a slow and ancient presence, full of empathy, surviving only to create more life. I thought nothing about it when living I greedily gobbled the ripe damsons warm in the July sun. Now I am the damsons, and the trunk that steadies the tree, and the branches that hold the birds with their delicate nests of precious eggs. I am tempted to spill them, watch them crack against my headstone, but the tree would be angry. It's such a righteous little thing, birthing life from rotten wood and dead leaves.

The tree bores me, even though I can see all around from the high branches. That's when I spotted the little girl. I willed her to come closer. Eyes screaming wide with hunger she plucked the juicy damsons. I pushed myself into them and bit by bit she consumed me too. The wizened old wood sprite shot me a warning, but I did not heed. I didn't want to spend my death locked in a tree. Now I'm inside her. I can feel her soul. It's young and afraid, easy to push aside. A voice calls my new name.

"Amelia, wicked child, come back at once." My new mother snatches my arm, and I shrug her off. She looks at me oddly. Her own daughter cowers in fear. Why are you so frightened? I ask, but she scuttles away, happy to hide.

"I'm sorry, Mother," I say, "but the damsons are so good." A sharp jolt snaps my head back and I realise she has hit me. I am sent to bed without any supper that night. The girl's spirit stays hidden and doesn't attempt to play with me. She's a weak, insipid thing. Her father came home late, and I know now why she quails with fright. Tomorrow I will return to the damson tree and choose my next body more wisely.

The dawn breaks gold behind the tree. A spirit shows its face, small and woody and before I know what's happening, the soul of the little girl is pulled deeply into a woody embrace, and I am left alone within her trembling body. Furious, I pound my fists against the bark. Then I hear her father.

"Amelia, you will pay for your disobedience. Come here now." Joyful giggles echo from the branches as Amelia and the wood sprite play together and I wonder why I never did the same.


Author note: My first attempt at flash fiction resulted in 'The Damson Tree.' At the time I lived in a house within a graveyard and would spend time with my cat Spook sitting on a pink marble grave under a tasty damson tree. The story emerged onto my notebook in scribbles stained with damson juice. It was first published in an online journal that is sadly no longer available, so has earned its place in my collection and speaks for itself.

# Transcending

I felt it arrive, squatting on the periphery waiting to pounce, catch me unawares, but I knew it was coming. My hair had begun to fall out, great tendrils trailing black and tangled in my hairbrush and blocking the sink. I changed shampoo, opting for natural vegan formulas, but it did no good. I decided to stop dying my hair, in case the dye was causing the hair loss. Now a few inches of coarse grey accentuate the bare scalp of my ever-expanding middle parting, my dark hair hanging floss-like in comparison.

Having been a thin person my entire life, I didn't expect the blubber that grew and hung from my middle. A pouch formed and expanded; now I sit bloated, spider-like, fretting and knitting with my scrawny arms. I knit to keep busy whereas I used to be active, but now my joints hurt, and I get tired so quickly. I catch a glimpse of myself in the reflection of the silent TV, hunched and hag-like. Shuddering, I place the knitting down and decide to shower, put some makeup on, tidy myself up.

Almost overnight my skin has sagged. I've always had laughter lines, but now they're more like grinning grooves and I have jowls. My features have collapsed, and the make-up I've always worn transforms me into a pantomime dame, both crass and cheap, a parody of my former self – the self I see inside my head, the self I've always recognised as me. The image that scowls back is not me, can't be me. I won't let it in. I return to my knitting, defeated.

I remember being pregnant with my daughter and on holiday in France. An old woman caught my eye in the market square of a provincial village. Crone-like, she sat sniggering and grinning, pointing to my small bump that was hardly showing as I was only about four months gone. I tried to avoid her gaze but found myself enclosed in a crush of people and pushed towards her table and wares. She spoke to me; my French was not great, so I feigned disinterest, but she grabbed my arm. Sun-browned fingers, old bone and sinew, curled gently but firmly, and her voice cackled, *Your baby will drink your beauty.*

I stepped back, shocked, but she turned her attention to selling some pickled preservative to a German man at my side, allowing me to scurry away. I've thought of what she said before but never felt it so much as now. I have been a young girl, pretty and carefree, and a mother, both vain and haughty, morphing into a different kind of beauty, an older confident beauty but still insecure. Now that mask is slipping, sliding away to reveal the truth, my truth, my transcendence into the final stage, the darker phase. The crone.

My daughter is a beautiful young woman, the embodiment of me at her age, but more confident with a sassy edge. She has moved away to live, a bright star in a darkening universe, while I have no energy for the dreams I hoped to fulfil. Dreams I believed I'd get back to one day in the future before I got too old. My cat Kafka curls on my lap stretching; a claw catches at my knitting, pulling a thread, destroying the pattern.

I watch the thread, the disruption, and quickly try to repair the damage. I unpick and start that row again, conscious of the unfurling wool, and feel my mind unfurling. I have forgotten what I was doing. *Mind fog* the doctor called it, and it comes with the menopause as well as all the other symptoms I am experiencing. I couldn't help finding the young GP attractive, and the knowledge that he probably has a young wife or girlfriend at home sickened me. I was once an attractive, sought-after young girl. Doesn't he realise this, with his looks of pity and condescending smile as he advises HRT? Can't he see what I once was? Can't he see through what I am becoming?

I begin to sweat. It stinks, sour and sickly, clashing with my perfume; even though expensive, it smells cheap and false. Nausea floods me, and I worry I will vomit. Dizzyingly, I get to my feet and remove my cardigan. I need air, so let myself into the garden. The fresh air cools my skin to goose flesh; a breeze pushes my stench around me, so I walk in a cloud of unseen odour, a constant reminder of my body's altering presence.

There is an old cherry tree at the bottom of the garden. The blossom is nearly past – it never lasts long enough. No sooner does it burst forth in beauty than a storm passes and ravages the delicate bouquets. The pink glory damp and browning with decay decorates the floor with a carpet of impermanence. I could sense it strongly, the thing that haunts me, squatting on spindly haunches watching, blossom stuck to its face with hair hanging in ratty tendrils.

I turn away, shun the feeling, suddenly cold, and hurry indoors; my knees click from the movement, reminding me of my condition. To call it a condition is wrong. It is a process all women go through, like puberty. I hadn't expected to feel so run down is all, I hadn't thought how losing my looks my body my youth my ability to reproduce to procreate… how losing this would leave me so vulnerable. I don't want it to happen; I don't want it to consume me.

Making a cuppa, I watch the thing watching me; it doesn't move, just stares. More blossoms descend to float around it before succumbing to the damp earth that claims all. I bite hard into a bar of chocolate, one of my only pleasures, and my bridge tooth comes loose. I curse my gluttony and quickly spit the bridge out. Regarding myself in the mirror, I smile. The gap shows as my reflection grimaces back. The thing in the garden cackles.

My daughter phoned to say she'd be coming to visit soon; her husband was busy working, and she had some news but wouldn't say over the phone. I'd already guessed; she was going to tell me she was pregnant. There was a change to her voice; a motherly tone had overridden the carefree flippancy of her usual conversations. Tears brimmed in my eyes, and I pretended I had no idea and was looking forward to seeing her because it had been too long. Thank God I'd already taken up knitting.

I felt better going to bed that night as talking to my daughter had cheered me. I'd opened a bottle of red wine and maybe drunk a little too much, but I'd gone off like a light. The dream that descended left me floundering. My work colleagues were cross because I'd been off work too long, so the boss came to get me. I struggled as he dragged me through darkness into a restaurant where a domed wood-burning stove glowed red. He folded me up like a ventriloquist's dummy and pushed me into the flames. People were laughing, and a chef with a hat and twirling moustache closed the oven door.

I woke screaming. The sheets were drenched in sweat, and my head throbbed feverishly. Kafka cat leapt from my bed and darted out of the door. I heard the cat flap release him into the night. I lay panting as, slowly, my body cooled to shiver against the now cold, wet bedding. I got up, changed my nightshirt, and stripped the bed. I put on a clean fitted sheet but couldn't be bothered to put on a clean duvet cover, so pulled it over me coverless. I lay there and listened for the thing in the garden. It had entered the house, I could hear it shuffling about downstairs and rummaging through my stuff.

That morning, I had a text from Jim asking if I wanted to meet up later. Jim was a divorced man in his late fifties with two grown up kids. We had been seeing each other for a few years. All had been fine until the last few months when I didn't seem to have any energy, and as for my libido, well, it was non-existent. Jim didn't get it, as we had been like teenagers before, but recently sex had become painful, and I kept getting thrush from various lubes and sex toys in a bid to reawaken things. I hesitated to reply but decided to invite him over; he said he'd take me out for dinner, so I didn't have to cook.

Whilst making a coffee I noticed rotten cherry blossom squashed across the floor of the kitchen and living room. I remembered the thing had been in the house last night. It had pulled out old photo albums and left them strewn across the settee, pictures of me as a young woman and then as a mother laughed at me. A plate and bowl were in the sink, so it had eaten. I sniffed the bowl and recognised the sickly-sweet scent of vanilla ice cream. I sat down on the kitchen stool and noticed my slippers had blossom stuck to the pink fluff. My eyes went to the cherry tree and the thing beneath it, crouching amongst the decaying flowers, waiting.

I spent ages deciding what to wear that evening for my date

with Jim. All of my clothes had ceased to fit overnight; my figure-hugging dresses revealed hip fat and a bulbous belly. In exasperation I pulled on an oversized blouse and leggings, ditching the idea of cinching the waist with a belt. As I considered how to apply makeup without appearing to have applied any, I noticed my gap tooth. How could I have forgotten? I couldn't go out like this, and if I wedged the bridge back in I wouldn't be able to eat without risking choking on it. I called Jim to cancel.

Jim, bless him, insisted that he didn't mind my gap tooth, but he didn't understand that I was the one who minded. Just because he liked me didn't mean I liked me. He suggested instead a takeaway of my choice, and he'd bring some wine. All I had to do was open the door when he arrived, and I could even wear my pyjamas if I wanted. I reluctantly agreed and chose Indian because I knew that was his favourite. I knew all he really wanted was sex. It was amazing the lengths men went to get it.

I didn't wear my pyjamas, leaving my blouse and leggings on in a bid to appear normal. He arrived on time as usual, amidst a cloud of spice and fried odours emanating from the carrier bag he held. He'd brought a couple of cold beers and a very good bottle of wine. He smiled, and I realised how lucky I was: he was an attractive man, even more so with his grey hair and he still kept his figure trim. Immediately I felt inferior and frumpish. What the hell is he doing here with a miserable fat, ugly, old cow like me? He entered, and I slammed the door on the cackling I knew would be coming from the cherry tree.

The evening began well, and I even felt my old libido return. One thing led to another, and we ended up in bed. We were both familiar with each other, but I was not familiar with what had happened to my body. It was not pleasurable, and I know Jim felt the change in me. It hurt when he touched me, and I was so dry I could feel my vaginal wall tearing even with the lube that just irritated. Thankfully the wine had dulled my senses, and I turned away from him when he'd finished and descended into a drunken sleep.

I woke to voices arguing. Jim wasn't in bed. I could hear his tones echo up the stairs. A voice not unlike my own but more frantic and screechy was replying, getting louder. Jim was trying to placate them, and a scuffle ensued. I hid, willing myself to become invisible as Jim entered the bedroom. He grabbed his clothes and went back downstairs. More scuffling was followed by a scream. Then I heard Jim say clearly, "You're mad. I've tried and tried but you need professional help." The other voice cackled, and I heard something metallic drop to the floor. The front door opened and slammed as something smashed against it from the inside.

I looked out of the window as Jim hurried down the garden path, struggling to get into his coat. I picked up the kitchen knife where it had fallen and cleaned up the smashed vase that had been hurled against the front door. There was cherry blossom stuck in the carpet and all over my slippers again. Long strands of greying hair were tangled in my fingers, and my scalp hurt where I had been tearing at it. I heard the cat flap, and Kafka entered; he brushed against my legs purring, and I began to cry.

I stopped taking the anti-depressants the doctor gave me and agreed to go on HRT. My daughter was coming to visit, and I wanted everything to be in order, including my brain. I'd been knitting booties in pale green, and baby blankets. I'd spoken to her again, and she'd practically confirmed my guess. I was going to be a grandmother. I looked at my reflection and tried to comb my hair over the bald patches that had formed since the night Jim had visited. I'd had one text from him: he hoped I was okay, and we'd better not see each other again, or at least until I got help.

The night before my daughter arrived, I went to bed early. I felt positive, more than I had for some time, although I was a little apprehensive about what she would make of my appearance. I'd still not had my bridge tooth replaced; it took forever to get a dentist appointment these days. Again, dreams flooded my mind, and I felt hot, burning hot. The sweat oozed out of my pores, the stench cloying and thick like fat from a roasting pig.

I opened my eyes to the smouldering interior of the domed nightmare oven. Scarlet skin blistered and tingled as I scratched and scrambled, twisting onto my stomach to push at the door. My hands burned, nails breaking like tinder, my hair a halo of fire as the heat roared, and scorching flames licked the soles of my feet, the pain burning up my calves. Screaming, I pounded and woke, scratching at my skin until red and inflamed it bled into the damp sweaty sheets.

Once again I changed the bedding. I was awake now and knew sleep would not return before dawn. Unable to decide if I was hot or cold, I left the duvet on the floor and simply lay upon the cool sheet. I could hear a noise in the hallway. A strange voice humming a tune and footsteps ascending the stairs slowly until they reached my bedroom door. Panicking, I tried to move but found I couldn't. Corded muscles constricted my throat as I struggled to grunt into movement, my breathing getting faster until erratic gasps leapt from my chest.

I felt the thing enter the bedroom. The same screechy, cackling voice that had screamed at Jim now muttered and cooed. Bony hands prodded my stomach, and the voice giggled, dry and rasping. I felt it circle the bed, watching me. Cherry blossom, rotten and decayed, dropped onto my nightshirt as it clambered over my body. The sour stench of sweat lingered as it passed before squatting by my feet. I looked into a face of wrinkled bark haloed by grey hair wisped sparsely over mottled skin, stretched tight over a skull, erect upon a sinewy neck.

I tried to kick it away, tried to get up and run, imagined myself doing this and putting on the light dispersing the nightmare, but every time I thought I'd woken I found myself back on the bed laid out like a feast. The heat returned, and I could feel myself burning up. I was back in the restaurant of my dream, displayed on a serving tray, still hot from the oven. The thing sat at the table waiting as silent hands and feet wheeled me closer. I passed other tables where my work mates grinned and raised glasses to me, and there was Jim with a younger woman that looked like I used to.

My feet tingled. The cooked skin blistered and flaked. The thing's nostrils flared and tasted my smell before looking to the chef with the twirling moustache and, smiling, thanked him. The others in the restaurant had stopped their chatter and watched as the thing picked up a serviette and draped it over their lap. It raised a glass of pink blossom to the onlookers, and I heard Jim's voice shout cheers before laughing, and the chatter resumed. The chef twirled his moustache with a flourish and returned to the kitchen.

A tongue shrivelled from a lipless mouth and slowly licked the dripping fat from the soles of my feet that twitched in reply. It smiled with a gap-toothed grin and opened its mouth, ingesting my toes one by one until my feet, too, slipped inside the slavering maw. I watched helplessly as the neck contracted to swallow my limbs like a python, the nose stretched wide, the jaw dislocated to receive my body. I swivelled my head towards Jim in a plea for help, but he was engrossed in conversation with the faceless beauty, her back turned firmly against me.

A scream ripped silently through my mind as I watched it slide upwards, devouring my lower self. Eyes like cherry stones widened in mock alarm as its mouth stretched wider to gorge on my stomach. Pointed elbows straddled either side as it clawed forwards with bulging throat to devour my torso and merge with my heart. The jaws closed into a pursed kiss to swallow before clamping over my neck. I tried to struggle to stop the inevitable as wet lips sucked at my chin.

Closing my eyes, I succumbed, gave myself over to the thing as it swallowed the self I would no longer be. The other people had finished their meals, including Jim; they began to leave the restaurant as birdsong dispersed the scene. I felt my breath exit my body in one great sigh before my head transcended and released into a crushing darkness. I lay there, sweat clammy on an old body, wondering what my daughter would think when she arrived to find this hag-like being that had consumed her mother.

Author note: 'Transcending' earned a place in an anthology called *Bodies Full of Burning* to raise awareness about the menopause, published by an American horror press, Sliced up Press, and edited by the marvellous Nicole M. Wolverton. She found my story terrifying and a difficult read… but then thought hey, it's horror! I wanted to show how the menopause can be all consuming, making you feel as if your life is over. The confusion and self-doubt topped up with night sweats, insomnia and depression can be crippling but in reality, you are transcending to a higher place. The cherry blossom symbolizes both life and death, yet is beautiful at the same time leading you to the beginning of another phase of existence: the crone.

# Sea Glass

Wind soughed through the dune grasses as black-backed and herring gulls screamed and scrabbled amongst the mounds of kelp and rubbish washed up by the tide. Crabs were plucked and pulled apart; the lucky ones scurrying to hide under stones or slip into the stillness of a rock pool. Sharp gusts of stinging sand roughened my cheeks, gritting my vision as the salty ocean air, carrying the smell of fish and seaweed, filled my lungs. The waves sucked backwards, the tide retreating, spent after the morning rush to deposit its load onto the shore and spew over the rocks.

I sat on a log of driftwood, partly burned where someone may have used it for a fire, or maybe lightning had broken it, scorching the wound, casting the limb far from its body, lost and forlorn and not dissimilar to how I'd been feeling since the loss of my mother, which had left me reeling and struggling to cope. A crushing sense of isolation and confusion swam to the forefront of my waking days, and I blinked away tears encrusted with sleep.

I came here often to try and process my part, or lack of, in her last days. I felt drawn by the old Victorian cast iron lighthouse, cemented into the rock. It lured me. My gaze pulled to take in its rusted facade; a once needed beacon left to deteriorate and decay, ignored by all except nature and now me as I pondered its descent into a discarded future.

My mother's suicide had been a shock. Fresh anguish erupted as I struggled to banish the image of her, separating myself from the emotions that seared me in two. Then I saw you, illuminated as the winter sun broke briefly, reflecting off the sea foam and churning opal swell. I observed your disheveled form wandering the tide line, stooping down, searching, collecting unseen things, examining them attentively, before secretly hiding them away in a raggedy bag that hung across your chest.

My hat was pulled down tightly and I removed it to feel the wind against my scalp. You were peering through something in your hand, glinting green, and that's when you saw me. Your scrutiny was disconcerting and although the cold air was not unpleasant, lifting and whipping my hair to obscure my features, I felt self-conscious, exposed and dissected, my inner self on display. Like you were inside me and knew all about me.

To avoid your gaze, I looked towards the estuary as it barged into the sea, and to the hazy land beyond the turbulent waters. The lighthouse obscured my view as it scowled, bracken-colored with rust, abandoned and unloved, the lamp extinguished long ago, except for a slight glint of jade that flashed once like an eye blinking into my mind, seeing what I could not and did not want to see for myself.

Quickly I pulled the woollen warmth of my hat back over my head and continued to avoid your gaze as you approached, your gait shambling and unsteady. I wanted to walk away because I felt unsure how to handle your intense scrutiny, but didn't want to appear impolite or selfishly arrogant, especially if you might be in need of help, yet something about you unsettled me. A knowingness, a gleam of recognition nudged at the barriers of my mind.

A herring gull landed at your feet to pluck at something I couldn't see, but you didn't remove your gaze, head tilting to one side as you stared. I tried out a smile and raised a hand as if in greeting, like I would to a friend, except you were not a friend, you were an anomaly, a mad thing making me nervous. Even the gull stopped his plucking to take in our exchange, grey wing feathers slightly darker than the winter sky. You shouted something but the wind snatched it from my ears.

I glanced to the side, away from you and up the beach where flat rock beds stretched into a craggy coast leaving the shifting dunes behind. I hoped you'd return to your beach combing and lose interest in me, but I could feel your form getting closer. You continued to approach until I could see your feet; bloodless and bare encrusted in damp sand, with brown cracked toenails, and had they not walked towards me I would have thought them those of a corpse. Maybe they were and you had collected them and placed them over your own.

I raised my gaze over faded cotton trousers, the colours once vibrant now dull and worn and somehow familiar, to a navy woollen jumper, stretched almost to your knees, misshapen with threads pulled revealing small holes where skin peaked. You were naked underneath, and I wondered how you did not freeze. Hesitantly, as I felt afraid being seated before you, I rose and stepped away.

Lifting your own gaze from below a hat of washed-out blue, pulled low over limp sandy hair, you stood taller to make eye contact. I smiled and said hi, my voice sounding foreign, my language unfamiliar. Lovely day, I continued feebly, glancing at the cold winter seascape. Your

head turned and you took in the same view, lingering over the lighthouse before returning to catch and this time, hold my eye.

Storm-coloured eyes, sheltered behind red wind-blistered lids framed by pale lashes, flickered in recognition as you absorbed my features. Sunken cheeks hung either side of a long nose, red at the tip, which ran in the wind. Mucous dripped and quickly you raised a hand to wipe it, sniffing as you did, whilst cracked lips split with small streaks of blood spoke.

"Elsa?" Your hand that wiped your nose rubbed against your trousers before reaching towards me with something nestled in your palm. "Is it you?"

I didn't take the glistening offer but stepped back cautiously stammering, "How do you know my name?" I looked around hoping to see other people, dog walkers or kids playing in rock pools, but the beach was empty except for a fling of dunlins playing tag with the waves and, far out on a rock, a silent cormorant. The lighthouse watched our encounter in its brown cape of rust until the sharp peep of an oystercatcher sounded a warning and brusquely I suggested *You must have mistaken me for another Elsa,* and turned to leave.

"No," you said, shaking your head, eyes squinting in the white sun. Deflated, you sat on the driftwood, your breath wheezing to a sob.

I felt awful, and softening, began to console you, making encouraging noises about accompanying you home. You babbled some nonsense about the lighthouse guiding you to me. I asked your name and you laughed, the sound blending with the screech of a gull. Your hands rummaged in the tattered bag spilling small bones mixed with shells and twigs and from your palm fell a pebble of frosted green sea glass. Brandishing it before you, it lit up with a beam and in wonder I looked to the lighthouse.

The bones and twigs scattered onto the sand, and I felt a jolt through my spine and shivered. Stammering a useless apology, I sprinted across the beach, back to the path through the dunes that led to the empty cluster of shops and a chippy. I couldn't remember taking it, but I could feel the sea glass digging into my palm. Breathless and trembling, embarrassed by my reaction, I glanced back at your lonely form waving at me from the half-burnt log. The lighthouse sat silent and sombre behind you, water lapping the stone apron, the tide forever restless.

I saw you often after that; you'd be standing on street corners raising a hand to wave and once you sat at the same table as me, crushed into a tiny cafe, until a stranger asked if they could take your seat and I nodded. A child saw you too; she stopped her bike and spoke with you, before turning to consider me. Her friends jostled around her laughing, wondering why she had stopped to talk to no one. I walked away knowing you would follow.

My boyfriend told me I was mad, psychotic even, *just like your mother* were the words left unsaid. He'd yell at me drawing his hands through his hair and almost weep begging me to seek help, to not face this thing alone. Maybe he didn't want to find me like I'd found her…cold and lifeless amongst empty bottles, the air sour with the stench of vomit.

"Elsa, please I can't live like this." And he'd gesture towards the empty place setting I'd laid at the table for you. Both of us stared blankly at his outburst as I fingered the sea glass thinking what strange bottle had it come from and what message had it carried, and was that message for me. I didn't know which of us he was referring to when he threw me out but you came too, as always, my shadow, my ever present self.

I didn't return to my previous life or my job but took to wandering the beach at night sleeping in the dunes. Slowly I was detaching from the thoughts and images that tormented and judged; the ignorance bringing respite. The light of the moon shone down on the lighthouse and I watched it, waiting for it to show me the way, to guide me, its rusty pallor stark in contrast to the watery sky that blended into the sea making it hard to tell where water ended and sky began, they were as one.

The man in the chippy took pity on me, handing out left over chips and sometimes crispy batter. He trialled me with a job but had to let me go saying I put the customers off. He told me to get help, or someone would call the police. I didn't know how to get help, and tried to ask you but you were drifting away from me. I saw you once in the eye of the lighthouse holding the sea glass so it caught the sun's rays. I ran towards you, but the sea swelled and pulled at my legs and fearing drowning I turned back, then when I looked up you were gone.

My memory dimmed every day, and I couldn't remember where I had come from or even my name. Soon I even stopped seeing you and a cold loneliness descended as winter drew in, taking the tourists back to their homes. I missed you so much my heart ached. I'd not made much effort at friendship, and my arrogance must have pushed you away. Had you gone somewhere new, a fresh start? Or back to wherever we'd come from, leaving me washed up by the tide.

Everything I had left of my life was in the tattered bag that hung across my chest. The sea whispered messages, swirling and flowing as I collected her gifts of shells, bones, twigs and there in the foam gleamed the pebbled green sea glass. Had you not held it last, lighting the beacon high in the lamp of the lighthouse? Had you dropped it into the sea for me to find or had you passed it to me as a gift?

I held it to the sun to watch the world through the frosted glow and saw a figure walk along the beach to stop and sit upon the half-burnt driftwood I had huddled by that night, freezing naked under my jumper. A nimbus of sandy hair whipped about her head before she pulled a blue hat down tightly stirring a memory, a memory I had once been.

"Elsa?" I called, but the wind took my voice.

I'd not seen you for so long that I hesitated to approach. I cursed myself for the times I'd ignored your waves and attempts at communication before pushing you away, believing my boyfriend when he said you were no one, that there was nobody there. A scene of scattered place settings crept to mind, a memory of who I once was, a grieving half-woman, but you were someone... you were not no one; you were all I had left of myself.

"Elsa!" I called again, shuffling towards your lonely form, holding out the sea glass, a gift of apology, a gift of knowing from the lonely and the lost. As I drew closer, I could see fear in your eyes, even as your hair buffeted, obscuring your features. I saw confusion and revulsion. "Is it you?" I asked, offering my gift in red cracked hands, sniffing and wiping my nose as it dripped. The lighthouse blinked green across the water flickering recognition in your expression, and I saw how you resembled me, or I you... maybe we were one and not two.

I told you to look to the lighthouse, let it guide you as it had me. I worried we'd become lost, trapped in the sea's ebb and flow until we were nothing but bones washed up on the tide. I offered the sea glass again but repulsed by me and my red scoured hands you stood saying I was mistaken. I collapsed onto the log, a wheeze of sadness escaping my chest and you softened, speaking patronizingly of taking me home, as though I was mad; a crazy half thing you feared. Then you ran and I followed.

I watched you ignore me at first and turn away, too absorbed in your suffering, but soon you accepted I was there, even laid a dinner setting for me and defended my existence to others. Then one day as summer stumbled into winter's embrace, I lost you, and believed you had started a new life leaving me alone on the beach. I searched for you, for a message or anything washed up by the tide. I wandered alone, hiding from the pain and grief that had torn me apart, splitting my presence in two.

Then I saw you, high up in the lighthouse and like a vision you beckoned. I splashed into the sea struggling against the pull of the tide calling to you. Look to the lighthouse, you cried, your voice blending with the crash of the waves. Let it guide you through this sea of madness, past the rocks of despair and home to the shores of yourself. I wanted so much to remember who I was, to join you and feel whole once more no matter what the cost. Tears blurring my vision, I held up the sea glass to catch the beam of light that flickered from your hand, and fighting the sea's ebb and flow I followed where the green ray shone.

Author note: This next tale has earned the special place of being the title of my anthology. 'Sea Glass' was first published by Eibonvale Press in an impressive collection entitled *At the Lighthouse* and published by the talented Sophie Essex. Eibonvale is an exclusive press that publishes the most beautifully designed hardback books, some limited editions, bursting with magical realism and the weird. 'Sea Glass' deals with the terrifying loneliness and bewildering devastation of mental illness. The lighthouse is a constant throughout, a beacon of hope, the green ray symbolic of healing and the tumbled sea glass a message and a link back to oneself.

# The Grundylow

I saw a grundylow in the pond at the bottom of my garden, where it turns muddy. I don't usually go down there, too many bugs and midges, but during the recent months of drought and sunshine the pond had dried up considerably. Pretty flowers scattered the banks, cowslip trumpets, king cups, and wild orchids now clustered the usually dank marshland, a rare splattering of color instead of murky brown and algae green.

Because of the drought, the bottom of the pond revealed itself like shattered brown crockery, dried up and shriveled. Towards the middle lay a slug of murk and damp. It was here that I saw it, the grundylow. Poor thing was half in and half out of the sludge, struggling to hide in the shallow puddle. Frog eyes narrowed and fish lips sneered away from pike teeth. The feeble display was pitiful.

I made soothing noises and sat still on the bank, watching. The grundylow gurgled and flapped, fear raising their hackles towards me. How things change. I remembered the old stories, how grundylows had dragged children to watery deaths, feeding on their flesh. My grandmother would hiss and snarl during the tales, reaching bony fingers to tickle us kids until we screeched and hid, fear and laughter close companions. It kept us safe – we steered clear of the waterways.

Jenny Greenteeth was the one we feared most, but she lived up north. Down here in the Welsh marshes we called the grundylows *mari morgans*. Men succumbed mostly. Addled with drink they mistook the grundylows for young women; they had sweet voices with which they sang, which is why children got caught too, believing them to be fairies or other kids. Nobody ever survived an attack, only chewed up bones making it home to stricken families.

I watched the grundylow struggle before deciding to approach. I couldn't help but feel sorry for the creature. I sat on my haunches on the cracked mud of the pond and reached out my hand. They scrabbled and tried to run before slumping into what little water remained, spent. My fingers brushed the top of their head where strands of pond weed, brittle and cracked, broke away. The grundylow was dying I thought, the drought was killing them.

I wanted to help. I couldn't just watch the creature shrivel and die before my eyes. Maybe I could coax them into the house and fill the bath with water. I'd get some water weed from the garden center, turn my bathtub into a pond, and keep the grundylow alive until the rains returned. I could feed them fish, but would draw the line at human flesh, although this thing looked too small to be a threat.

"Hey, Grundy," I whispered, "don't be scared. I'll help." I tried to lift the creature, feeling sharp spines along their back. They flinched and hunched away, hiding something. I could hear a sweet song, the voice of a young girl rising around me before cracking. Gently I gathered the bag of spines and bones into my arms, helping them to sit up – and noticed then what was clutched in the creature's arms.

A tiny grundylow peered at me. The baby had been suckling a dry, flappy teat. Green liquid oozed from the side of a slitted mouth. The infant hiccupped before beginning to cry. The sobs broke my heart. I had found a female grundylow with her young. This was rare. I didn't know how grundylows reproduced, but obviously they must do – wasn't that tragic beast Grendel the child of one? I had to help this poor female and her suckling babe.

I told her she must trust me and explained about the bath. She stared, head-cocked, and I think she was beginning to understand. I held out my hand and tentatively she placed her husk-like fingers in mine while her other arm cradled the whimpering tot. She was very weak, and I could hear her breath wheezing in the dry air. What looked like gills in her neck closed stiffly, caked in mud.

I walked slowly, leading her down the garden. Thin, webbed feet blistered in the sun. I knelt down to her level and explained I needed to carry them both the rest of the way. The grass was hot and the garden path burning. She twitched from foot to foot before reaching a spindly arm around my neck, allowing me to lift her as she clutched her baby.

Her body was like a sack of sticks and twigs that smelled, not unpleasantly, of mold and earth. The usual pond stench of a grundylow had long dried up, leaving a sweeter fragrance. The spines along her back were sharp, and I was careful not to cut myself – I didn't want her to get a whiff of human blood. She was still a wild and dangerous being.

My hip nudged the back door, and I carried her through the cool stone-flagged kitchen and into the bathroom. I placed her in the tub and ran the cold tap. She adjusted her baby and blinked her relief, eyelids sticking to jellied eyes. Water swirled around her limbs, the dust and sludge coloring it woody brown. Her skin began to soften; dry patches flaked off, floating to the surface. She sighed and lowered herself into the water, stretching out. The baby kicked and woke, then began swimming newt-like around her.

"I'll get food," I said, "and some pond weed. I won't be long, try to rest." She regarded me, eyes bright with gratitude. I smiled and her lips grimaced in response.

There wasn't much choice of pond weed in the garden center, the plants were dry and in as much need of rehabilitation as my grundylow. I bought what they had, and picked up some fresh cod from the fishmongers on the way home. I asked for any fish they were throwing out, saying I had a cat that needed feeding up. The stench made me gag in the hot car on the way home.

Half of me wondered if she'd still be there, or had she replenished herself and slunk away to the marsh? The other half wondered if I'd dreamed her, a hallucination from too much sun. Cautiously, I approached the bathroom door. Small sounds cooed from within, a young woman's voice, childlike and dainty. I opened the door to the juxtaposition.

She was returning to her old form, the water giving her life. More dead skin coated the bathtub and floated string-like. Underneath, fresh skin glowed greenish, her eyes had regained their bulbous watery stare, and her gills opened and closed freely. The strands of hair left on her head draped over her chest, where the little one suckled greedily. The tiny head was oval and smooth, larger than their green body, which was furred moss-like, with twiggy arms and legs.

I removed the pond weed from the pots and placed them into the bath; she watched me like Ophelia amongst the fronds. She was beautiful I realised. I was aware she might be spelling me, but I was a woman like her and, according to legend, women did not succumb in the same way as men. She was simply a beautiful creation, and I marveled at her.

I gave her the fish, even the fresh cod, my own appetite having retreated from the stench. Eagerly she snatched them, disappearing under the water. She fed underneath and I could hear sounds both savage and sweet. I waited patiently until she resurfaced. I could tell she was ashamed, but I smiled encouragingly, telling her she had to eat to get strong to feed the little one. Her lips pulled back from her teeth and she gripped my arm. I flinched but her grip was gentle and doll-like as she squeaked a thank you.

I stayed with her for most of the night. I told her my name was Gwen; she grimaced a smile and told me hers was Jilly. I remembered that name; it belonged to a missing child from years ago. I asked her how she'd got her name, and she said she didn't know, but most mothers took the names of their victims to give to their children. I asked what she'd called her little one, holding my breath for the answer, hoping it wasn't another missing child.

"Lamb," she said. "His name is Lamb." She explained how the poor, bleating creature got separated from its mother, and she had taken the fragile life. She'd been heavily pregnant, and the drought had weakened them both. Soon after she had given birth, the lamb's blood gave her the strength she needed. Grundylow births are complicated; many mothers do not survive the process.

Jilly and Lamb lived in my bathtub for the whole summer. Lamb got larger, and I worried about them being discovered. I had recently broken up with a boyfriend, and he'd come around a few times hoping for a reconciliation or sex. I'd hidden in the bathroom giggling, ignoring his knocks and calls, Jilly's girlish voice joining my own. He must have got the message in the end, through the sound of splashing water and female shrieks. I hoped we'd made him jealous.

In reality, my bathroom was far from a feminine boudoir: it stank. Jilly was loath to change the water, preferring the stagnant green and smelly sludge to fresh. She also liked to leave the fish guts floating about for Lamb to wallow in, and practice eating solid food. I understood it was her habitat, and how she liked it. I, however, had taken to washing with a flannel at the sink.

My friends began to ask questions. I visited their houses but always put them off from coming to mine. Now I just stayed in – it was easier, and I preferred being with Jilly and Lamb anyway. I knew they would have to move back to the marsh when the rains came, so I wanted to make the most of our time together. I would miss them. I enjoyed Jilly's company and even cuddled Lamb when she needed some peace. She knew she'd have to leave soon too; a murky bathtub was no place for a young grundylow to grow up.

September drew to a close and the sky darkened, heavy and brooding. The weathermen predicted thunderstorms and torrential rain. Flood warnings were issued and people piled sandbags outside their front doors. I didn't need to tell Jilly the news; she could smell the rain coming. Her nostrils flared as lightning lit, thunder crashed, and pattering drops began to pour before pregnant clouds released a deluge.

She rose from the bathtub, goddess like, carrying Lamb on her hip, his twig legs clutching, and walked through to the kitchen. I opened the door. The rain glistened silver in the lamp light, and she stepped into the torrent. I followed her to the pond, my own clothes plastered to my back. The pond was beginning to fill rapidly, and I could smell a mineral-rich dampness from the marshy waters beyond.

Lamb was kicking and yipping with excitement. She released him into the pond, and we watched as he swam and leaped, twirling and diving. He peeped from the surface, bug-eyed and grinning. Sharp teeth were beginning to form, two at the top and one below. It gave him a gap-toothed innocence. We laughed at his antics, proud parents.

I touched Jilly's soft arm scales, fingers trailing a shiver to her neck. She breathed sharply, reaching for me. Pad-like fingertips cupped my face. I rubbed my cheek against her cold, clammy palm. Her hair had grown back, framing her face in emerald weed. Leaning forward she pressed amphibian lips to my own. I wrapped my arms around her, gasping as a sharp scale caught my finger. She held my hand and sucked the wound; concern creased her face as she recognized my fear. Smiling she released my hand and kissed me again, pulling me close.

Her body felt firm and wet, the brittleness healed, fresh skin and muscle returned. She had grown taller, almost matching my own height. Even her breasts felt soft, and her belly small and rounded once more. Sharp teeth trailed over my lips, and she breathed my scent before slipping from my grasp.

"Wait," I cried. "Will I see you again?"

Eyes bright, quicksilver hands lifted from the pond in farewell. I watched two shapes dart otter-like into the shadowy depths, and out through the overflow into the marsh.

Reluctantly I returned to my own life. Loneliness prevented me from cleaning the bathroom as I longed for her presence. The neighbour complained of a boggy smell and, unable to put it off any longer, I got to work. The stink was getting to me too if I'm honest. I bagged up the fish guts for the rubbish, and took the pond weed down to the bottom of the garden to plant.

Pressing fragile roots into the squelch of the bloated pond, I called her name. My voice echoed emptily over the marsh. Wading birds had returned; they rose startled into the sky sounding a caterwaul of shrieks. I sat in the weak autumn light watching the pond. Ripples formed, bubbling and spreading. Reeds parted, swirling in the greenish depths, and a delicate childish singing rose from beneath. Showing no fear, I waded eagerly into the water as the surface broke with a splash, and the song of a grundylow washed over me.

Author note: I chose a Grundylow as my cryptid of choice for a submission call to an American anthology, *Dark Cheer, Cryptids Emerging: Volume Silver* by Improbable Press and edited by the fantastic Atlin Merrick. This is a world where the mysterious merges with the everyday and an unlikely love story evolves, or is the creature simply behaving as is their nature? The nature of the beast…

# Alderwood

The estate agent shied from the wind that tugged her hair, and bristling against the wintry fingers, she rushed to meet me before indicating the house. Our voices were carried into the branches of the alders that swayed along the riverbank. The door opened before bracing against a pile of junk mail and with a shove we passed into the relative shelter of an empty musty kitchen.

"As you can see, it needs some work but it's structurally sound." She glanced at my initial reaction which I hid with a smile. "You're aware you can't really change anything, only decorate to your own taste, which should be fun." Her heels clipped on the flagstone floor, false smile firmly in place. The gusting rain splattered against the single-paned windows making her jump ever so slightly.

The terms of sale stated that the house was not to be altered due to its age and green belt location which included extensions, extra levels or walls coming down. No builders were going to bully their way around this special place. It had taken me a long time to find it, but now I had, the resurrection could finally begin. I had travelled a long way for this.

An inglenook dominated one wall of the kitchen where an old stove, complete with oven, hulked, the iron cold and dusted with cobwebs. In the corner something stirred, a rattle of bones jerked and tired eyes peered from the dark. The old Domovoi house spirit was still here, I noticed. The estate agent saw me looking and flapped her hands; embarrassed, she said, "It's been empty for some years now, needs a bit of love. I'll get someone to check for vermin."

"Its fine," I said, watching the old thing scuttle behind the stove, movements jerking, breath wheezing until it was absorbed by the iron once more. "I'll take it as it is." I surprised myself at how forthright and confident my voice sounded. "There haven't been any other offers yet, have there?" I was sure there wasn't, but others had searched for this place.

"No, nothing, which is a shock as it's such a quaint little place. It's the inability to do any large renovation that puts people off these days. Everyone wants to transform these old places into modern mansions."

"Well, that's something I'm not interested in and I'll pay the asking price, so take it off the market today?"

"Asking price?" Her eyes lit up. "Oh yes, I should be able to secure it for you. Do you want to have a wander around and I'll make a call and get it sorted? I'll have to go back to the car as the signal isn't great inside these thick walls."

I watched her disappear through the heavy oak door glancing over her shoulder at the squall of rain hurling itself in pursuit. A slender birch guarding the gate whipped its silver branches in her wake eager for her to make the call. Eyes stared from behind the stove watching as, smiling, I ran my fingers over the stone feeling no damp, just cold, and waited.

"Congratulations, you're the new owner of Alderwood, or Ty Gwernen which it used to be called in Welsh," beamed the estate agent.

The pretty name derived from a ragged tangle of alder trees that ranged along the banks of the river that ran by the base of the hill. They crept up the bank to end in one tall, wrinkled trunk dotted with lichens. The rest of the wood waltzed and entwined its way either side of the stream, dancing through the wetland until deeper into the forest, oak and ash took over.

Alder trees form a gateway to that other place, the land of twilight where the fey linger and roam passing between the realms. It was the alders that had guided the house to rest in this spot, its crooked little legs all spent, bleeding and cracked as it fled from war, fire and persecution. It had come to rest on protected land, land where nature had been allowed to thrive, protected from the eyes of the estate that owned it and nurtured by the locals. Soon its overnight arrival became nothing but an old wives tale and the old witch, yet to arrive from a land far away, simply a fairy tale.

My few meagre pieces of furniture were delivered the same day the keys were handed over, well key, as there was only one, heavy and cold with the frost of a thousand winters. My memory wandered into those northern forests, and I shivered remembering the penetrating cold, wrapped in fear, smothered with the pain and tears of suffering and death. I watched the white van drive away over the bumpy track, the driver and his muscle assistant happy with their wad of cash.

"On your own love?" he'd asked. "Seems a bit remote."

"I like it," I'd replied. He didn't need to know the real reason behind my move, and as for remote, this was nothing compared to where I came from. The tail end of the van turned on to the lane, and I listened to the engine fade until the sounds of nature took over unfolding unseen arms around me, and I relaxed.

\*

"What do you think of her then?" asked the muscle in the passenger seat, glancing in the wing mirror at the distant woman, blond hair billowing, beautiful face pale against the stark forest backdrop.

"Seems nice enough to me."

"I'm not sure why a looker like her would want to live all the way out here though, unless she's up to no good."

"Don't be ridiculous Aled, and don't you dare go snooping round there either."

"What do you mean? I don't snoop. That place is too bloody creepy for snooping; maybe the old witch will come and scare her off."

"You remember the old tales then?"

"Not really, just always been known as the witch house hasn't it?" said Aled, nervously glancing over his shoulder at the dark track.

"She won't last long. Probably a writer or something and needs somewhere quiet for a bit. Hopefully we'll be moving her things back out again come winter." Both men winced as the van bumped over a particularly large rut in the long track back to the lane.

\*

I was far from my native land and so was the house. I wondered if the old legs, nestled beneath the foundations, could still walk. The memory of another place brushed against my mind: from another country altogether the house had fled, to this land of myth and legend. Wales. A forgotten place itself but here the house had rested safely, far from danger and far from those seeking to destroy *her* and steal *her* power.

I'd chosen the smaller of the two bedrooms and hung my few clothes in the wardrobe that had come with the cottage, an old lump of dark wood which smelt of evergreen forests. I placed my childhood doll on the bed; although silent, I still hoped to hear her voice guide me through the darkness. A small window overlooked a tangle of brambles, but I could see the path down through the alders to the river, from where, exhausted, the house had emerged. Thankfully it had made it to higher ground.

The main bedroom was kept for *her* and it was on an ornate dressing table carved with fey creatures that I placed the pestle and mortar, an ancient object I'd found in a pawn shop in Poland. It had flown far away, disguised and worthless until I'd felt the pulse of magic as my hand cradled it and I knew.

I looked out over the front garden where the birch tree grew. A circular mound surrounded the house which I planned on uncovering in the hope of finding the remains of the boundary fence. The birch tree and fence were part of the essence of the place, as was the Domovoi, and I was happy to see that they had made it, materializing into place as the house settled. I wondered if the others would make it too.

I returned to the kitchen and began to light the old stove. It was late summer but there was a chill to the evening, and I was not used to being without a fire. The house too would be pleased with some warmth. There were plenty of logs which, thankfully, the estate agent had arranged delivery of. I smiled as lighting the match reminded me of how long ago I had risked so much for the gift of fire, but it had been worth it. With today's modern heating people had no idea how death stalked those with no fire in the frozen wasteland of the north.

I sat back on the old wooden rocker I'd brought with me, something I had guarded for many years and pulled a throw over my legs. Eyes shone from the flames and as I tapped my knees the old Domovoi sprang forth to curl onto my lap.

Relieved, I stroked his coarse skin until it softened into the wool of my throw, and a contented thrum reverberated from his throat and we slept.

When I woke the Domovoi was tending the fire. He would keep it lit both day and night, like his kind had done for centuries. I poured a bowl of milk and placed it on the hearth before ascending the stairs to bed. I wasn't tired but I needed my strength for *her* when *she* came back. I could feel *her* pushing on the periphery, skulking at the edges of time and space, just waiting for me to fulfill my side of the bargain.

*She'd* made me immortal but killed my entire family. It was what they deserved; *she* had told me… even my foolish father who was too weak to see through the spell my stepmother and sisters held over him. He turned his back on their bullying towards me and the cruel plan that forced me into the cold to seek *her* out and earn the fire that secured my survival. I had watched helplessly as they perished in the flames spewed forth from the burning skull.

\*

After a brew of bitter herbs to banish the sleep of night, I headed into the garden to start work on finding the fence under all the earth and weeds. The birch tree danced and sang in the breeze, his voice a sibilant swishing as he whispered encouragement. I smiled, stroking his gleaming trunk and watched him shiver from my touch. It was as I hoped. Under the earth, thorny bramble and stinging nettle, the rounded curve of a skull gleamed.

Slowly I uncovered the rest of the bones and skulls that had enclosed the house and garden and began to rebuild the boundary fence. I didn't care what others thought; soon people would be too afraid to pass this way, and God would not help those who did. As it was, the brambles and dog roses hid some of the grisly display for now, and by winter *she* would be here, to reclaim *her* cottage in the woods. I dare not think of what my own fate would be.

Pleased with my work, I walked down to the river to paddle my feet. There the water spirits stirred at my presence, crowding me, their liquid features both afraid and in awe of the being that lurked in my shadow. *She* is not yet strong enough, I told them. I assured them not to fear *her*, *she* had no problem with nature, but they could sense *her* ancient power and understood *she* was their guardian.

Walking back through the alders I stopped to watch the house. It had awoken. Slowly it began to shuffle and rise, creaking and shaking itself like a hen. Two rickety legs appeared and stretched from beneath as long chicken feet splayed and gripped at the earth. I clapped, laughing, and quick as a flash it spun around to face me. For a moment my heart caught in my throat as an old fear rose.

The eyes of the Domovoi flashed from the window as the house took a step forwards. I held my ground, my breath harsh and gasping. Closing my eyes, I stilled my erratic heart, quelling the fear. Soon, I reassured it, *she* will be here soon. Satisfied with the scrutiny of my innermost thoughts it turned, returning to its proper place, the legs curling underneath to rest once more, nestling into the earth.

\*

"Fancy another?" Aled glanced at Stu. They'd been drinking for most of the day. It was the village harvest festival and end of summer frivolities. The local brewery had its own stall on the village green. Families sat picnicking and playing games, children laughed, and dogs barked. Aled's boss Rhys had won the best grown cabbage section, and his wife had taken the flower arranging title for the third year running. Aled and Stu didn't contribute to anything, apart from lining the brewery's pockets.

"Aye go on then," answered Stu, "not much else to do, is there." Aled asked for two more pints and looked around.

"Who you looking for?" asked Stu.

"Just that woman from the old house in the woods, you know the one Rhys and me helped move."

"Bit of a looker you said, fancy your chances do you?"

"Christ no, too weird for me, I was just wondering if she was here. I've not seen sight nor sound of her since she arrived."

"Is she here then?" asked Stu looking across the green at a bunch of young girls.

"No, she's not. Probably thinks she's too upper-class to mingle with the likes of us."

"We'll have to head out there one evening. Check on her, in a neighbourly way, like."

"If I'm honest that place gives me the creeps. I just don't get how a young woman, and she's a proper smart looking piece of ass too, would be holed up out there all alone."

Stu raised his glass and drank some more. "Then maybe we should have ourselves a bit of fun, give her some company and teach her some respect, what do you think?"

Aled dismissed Stu's lurid remark and continued drinking his pint. Stu worried him; he'd spent time inside for sexual assault, apparently. Nobody else in the village knew this, but he'd told Aled, almost bragged about it.

\*

I placed more milk next to the oven and jumped as a black cat leapt from my chair and began lapping. Quickly I filled another bowl for the Domovoi. The cat stretched and purred, rubbing against my legs before strolling through the open door. I followed to watch it curl up in the sun on the stone path. The time is nigh I thought, ignoring the doubts and fears that arose about my own fate. This was what I had been waiting for, preparing for all these years.

I made a rich beef stew for strength and was just about to savor the last spoonful when frantic barking and scratching at the door disturbed me. The cat leapt to the window and stared, hissing a warning. Shut up, I told her; you knew he'd make it too. I opened the door for a scruffy rangy mongrel that scooted inside to warm itself by the stove. I gave him the last spoon of stew and watched his tail thump against the floor.

\*

The fever came first, causing nausea and sickness. I went down the stream to drink the cool waters of life; the spirits there greeted me with concern and urged me to return to the house. Their excitement was evident in the sparkling faces that swirled in the water. The birch tree swished impatiently. *Hurry hurry* came his urgent voice pushing through my sluggish mind. My body was resisting like *she* said it would, but there was no going back, I had signed my fate. I had enjoyed my many years on this earth still cloaked in the skin of my youth; now it was time to pay my dues.

Inside the house both cat and dog looked up expectantly before returning to slumber on seeing only me. The Domovoi crept forth, fat and plump now, to place a kiss upon my hand, his lips warm and moist. He had always shown kindness. House spirits were not generally renowned for their wickedness, even the ones who took care of witches' houses. Smiling in sadness I realised I could delay no further and began to prepare like I had been told – *her* impatience was evident. Upstairs, the pestle and mortar waited.

I drew the sacred sigils on the floor and lit the candles. Red for fire I placed south by the hearth, blue for water I put near the old sink in the west, silver for air I stood below the open window north of the hearth and green for earth I placed lastly on the stone floor to the east. I placed myself in the center, along with the pestle and mortar. I was spirit.

Taking a deep breath, I held my doll to my heart hoping to hear the voice of friendship guiding me as I had been guided so long ago. The voice had advised me through all the tasks placed upon me, but now the doll was mute. I knelt on the flagstones and calmly recited the words *she* had imprinted on my mind and then waited to fulfill my bargain. I had lived a long and prosperous life; it was time to welcome *her* home.

A whooshing came first, a surge of energy flickering the candles. The pestle ground and pounded against the mortar stone. I closed my eyes as it lifted into the air and began to circle me. The wind rose extinguishing the candles, plunging the small kitchen into darkness, only the glowing eyes in the embers remaining. Lightning flashed in the sky followed by a night-splitting crack of thunder that shook my skull, and I keeled forward onto the cold stone.

I could hear *her* voice; *she* crooned and muttered my name. Vasilisa my beautiful one, my faithful sister, rise and look at me. I struggled to stand, pressing my hands against the stone floor which vibrated and spun until shaking I staggered to my feet, held by legs that had no earthly feeling. Darkness and fire leapt all around and the rich scent of earth mingled with wood smoke, rot and decay. *She* sat before me on the rocking chair, the cat curled on her lap, long fingers stroking the head of the dog that sat by *her* side.

"Come closer," *she* whispered.

I approached *her* hag-like form; hunched and stinking *she* took my hand and like the Domovoi before *her*, *she* kissed it but did not stop there. Slowly *she* dragged *her* mouth across my skin. I watched *her* blackened tongue peel away my pale skin to coat *her* cracked and bleeding lips until my white bones gleamed through the viscera and *she* began to consume my very being.

Frozen, I listened to *her* murmurings and watched myself shrivel and shrink to a corpse before dissolving into nothing. Yet strangely I could still see myself. Sitting in the old rocking chair with the cat on my lap holding my doll and smiling as if we had just shared a joke. The cat's purring blended with my palpitating heart until it left my chest and flew forth, just a fluttering moth in the night rushing to burn in the light. The pestle and mortar stopped spinning and came to rest on the floor and began to grow, the stone groaning and rumbling to sing with the storm.

\*

"Where are you lads going?" shouted Rhys as he headed home with his wife, but there was no stopping them. He knew where they'd be headed, all full of booze. Hopefully they'd safely crash the van before reaching Alderwood and wake up with headaches. He felt the weather change as the van drove off, both lads laughing, pretending not to see him.

The wind whipped and whistled as a storm awoke, and Rhys toyed with the idea of calling the police, but it was so much bother these days, and to be honest he hoped Aled and Stu would have a good fright and leave the woman alone in future. There was no harm in them; well not Aled anyway. Stu was another matter.

\*

"Fuck, this is a hell of a storm," said Stu, high on adrenaline and beer. They'd parked out of sight at the end of the track and were sneaking up on the house from the back.

"Shhh. It's in darkness," said Aled. "Maybe she's gone away for the weekend."

"Hey, we can have a rifle through her things, see what she's hiding."

"No Stu, that's not right. I'm only here to see if she's okay."

The alders creaked in warning as out of the gloom the bone fence reared, skull jaws clacking.

"What the hell?" exclaimed Stu. "Is it Hallowe'en?"

"We'd better get out of here." Aled's voice quivered as a cold river of memory trickled through his mind and stories from childhood began to surface through the fog of alcohol. Stories that terrified; eldritch tales of witches and ghoulish spirits that lived in the forest where you should never ever go, lest you be caught, tortured and roasted alive. Slowly retreating Aled tripped on a fallen branch, a dog began to bark, and the house started to shudder. It bristled and shook as it slowly began to move, first turning right and then left as if scanning the woods.

"Fuck...It's moving, b– b– but how's it doing that?" stammered Stu, looking over his shoulder at Aled's terror ridden face.

"Just run Stu, bloody run man," Aled shouted as he stumbled through brambles and bracken, running blindly in the direction of the van. Stu stared at the house, his mouth an open cave of shock as he watched it rise up and spin to face him. A long scabby leg tipped with black claws scratched at the earth in anticipation of a chase Stu knew he would lose.

Shaking with panic he tried to run, yelling for Aled to wait up, embarrassed at how high pitched and girly his voice sounded. He felt warmth on his thighs and realised he'd pissed himself. The stench of beer sodden urine caught in his throat as he gasped with exertion, wet denim chaffing his skin as his legs fought with the undergrowth. Looking back, he saw a shadow and heard a whooshing noise followed by a thud thud thud coming from the house.

Skidding through the leaf mulch, Aled hesitated briefly when he heard Stu screaming and narrowly avoided a heavy pestle that shook the ground. A giant mortar hovered alongside Stu and in it brandishing the pestle like an oar, a pale woman shone with an ethereal glow, another form flickering within. An old hag wizened and twisted with a toothless mouth agape laughed. Like a bad TV signal, the image flitted from beauty to horror. The thing was gaining on Stu who seemed mired down by the forest floor that reached up, tangling his legs.

Transfixed, Aled watched as Stu fell, bashed from behind with the giant pestle and was lifted into the air. His terrified form hung upside down and dangling, lit up by a flash of lightning, hands grasping for help. Through tears of fear Aled tried to grab his friend's hands, when large bony fingers gripping tight to Stu's leg twisted him away, the sound of sinews tearing blending with a girlish giggle that ended in a crone's cackle. Feebly, Stu reached once more for Aled, eyes pleading, his face a bloody mess, but Aled had seen something else. The house was coming towards him. Through the trees it rushed, shrugging them aside to stride in the witch's wake.

Aled fell twice, his feet slipping and sliding in the mud as he ran, determined to save himself and reach his van, but the witch had stopped; her prey had been caught, and both she and the house retreated into the woods, the darkness folding gently over them. Aled retched onto the forest floor, fumbling for his keys. Letting out a quivering breath he scanned the trees, still ready to believe it all some crazy hallucination, except where was Stu? He whispered Stu's name, his voice breaking, but only the screech of an owl replied. His hands shaking, he started the van, and as the storm abated drove to Rhys's house.

"We gotta help him Rhys!" yelled Aled. "She's got him, the bloody witch bashed him with a giant pestle and picked him up, I saw him screaming and dangling all broken and bloody. Then the house, it… oh fuck man… it ran after us, I'm telling you it did." He rubbed his eyes aware that his telling of events sounded ridiculous, and he began to wonder if Stu had put something in his drink and if so then what in God's name had he just witnessed?

"Aled, calm down, you've had a lot to drink son. Listen to me. Remember those old stories? Your Mam must have told you about that old house, how we should stay away from it and that someday the witch would be coming?"

"Christ Rhys, we've not got time for fairy tales man, Stu's been taken by something. We got to call the police." But he did remember the stories – at least now he did.

"And tell them what you've just told me?"

"Fuck Rhys, what the hell am I gonna do? I gotta call them, Stu needs help but what am I gonna say?"

"Nothing. You're going to say nothing." Rhys stared hard. "Do you understand, lad?" Rhys never raised his voice, and this stunned Aled almost as much as what he'd seen. "Those stories are all true, son. I never thought I'd live to see it myself, but the witch is here. She's made it to Alderwood from whatever hell she's been dwelling in."

"What the hell do you mean the witch is here?"

"Think son, remember the tales?"

Aled screwed his face up. "But they're just folktales, stupid stories about a witch from far away and the house that appeared over night that the legends say walked here…" His voice trailed to silence.

"Yes son, there's always truth in the old tales," said Rhys. "We are *her* keepers now. It's our job to watch over *her* and make sure nobody finds *her*. *She'll* feed the earth and the water, and the village will prosper. Think about it, we'll not want for nothing lad, our crops will flourish, our veggies will be the best for miles around. All we have to do is keep *her* safe. You hearing me, son?"

"B – b – but what about Stu?" stammered Aled.

"He wasn't from round here was he, not born here. We all know *she'll* take a life from time to time, sometimes more often than not, that's what *she* does, the stories tell us that. We just got to make sure *she* gets enough outsiders is all, a few holiday makers now and then, an unfavorable sort here and there, what harm can it do as long as it's not one of us, eh?"

\*

Baba Yaga, or Ceridwen as she was referred to in Wales –

although her many names meant little to her – returned to her house in the woods pounding the ground with her pestle. Inside the mortar a slovenly form cowered and whimpered; shushing it with a slap she dragged it behind her. The birch tree greeted her with a lingering stroke of his silver boughs. The little gate opened as the moon peered forth from behind the clouds. The skulls grinning from the fence were washed clean by the late summer storm and shone in the moon's pale tears. Dog and cat ran to meet her. Dog yipped his excitement and cat purred; both knew fresh meat was coming.

The Domovoi knew this too, because smacking his lips he stoked up the fire until the stove belched heat, the oven white hot. Tonight, thought the witch, once I've feasted on flesh, I will sleep in my own bed once more. This land of myth and legend, steeped in folk tales and superstition will guard me well. Entering her house, she sighed in contentment and lighting a candle she watched as a moth awakened by the flame rushed towards it. Fluttering too close the wings burned, and the tiny body fell to the floor, singed and lifeless.

"Thank you, Vasilisa," she said, and catching a glimpse of her reflection in the cottage window, she added, "you truly are very beautiful." Then she kicked still the weeping form at her feet and began to select herbs and vegetables for the pot.

Author note: Baba Yaga is my favourite fairy tale character. She is the ultimate old woman and crone. I want her house to be my house! What a joy to have such a place. I imagined the house complete with its very own Russian version of a guardian spirit or Brownie, a *Domovoi,* coming to Wales. Vasilisa comes too, having made an agreement to find and care for the house and create the ritual that pulls Baba Yaga herself back from the darkness to her cottage once more. The villagers know, for it was written in legend, and they intend to benefit from her presence – for a price. The alder trees symbolise sacrifice, resurrection and immortality and in Welsh traditions they are a balance of both the masculine and feminine energies. Living next to water and swampy land signifies boundaries and is a link between the Otherworld or faerie realm and ours.

# Poor Ole Annie

The mountain cowered as the town birthed up fern clad slopes. Only the marsh escaped; a wild pocket of reeds and grasses where a deep tidal river slugged its way through. It was in this magical place amongst the chattering of reed warblers and the silent gaze of herons that I found my return home. An old Victorian farmhouse offered a wealth of character, not lovingly restored, just unchanged. Not even eighties glamour had influenced the decor over the years, and I liked it. It smelt old and breathed, expanding and contracting to inhale the salty marsh air.

There was a walled graveyard on the marsh, ancient and forgotten, an abandoned place of solace shrouded by nature. My Aunt Annie used to bring me here as a child. She told me that if I ran around a grave seven times, I would hear the body stir and speak beneath. I chose a simple headstone cushioned in moss with coffin shaped kerbs and footstone, a cozy grave, snuggling near the path.

I ran carefully once, then twice and kept going, but on the sixth turn a blackbird skittered a warning, flying low between the trees. The land tilted, my eyes swam with dizziness and almost falling I clutched my head. Watching the ground return to normal I decided not to make the seventh turn. The old bones of Mrs Thomas and her child, cradled in roots since 1785, could rest on. My aunt laughed saying I was a wise little girl and hugged me so tight I couldn't breathe. We picked wildflowers for mother on the way home.

These days the old church has long since been moved to a museum of buildings. Dating from the sixth century, it had been dismantled stone by stone. Underneath its drab protestant gown, bright medieval artwork blared. Experts, amazed at the discovery, painstakingly restored St Catherine, St Christopher, and the Passion of Christ complete with the Holy Father. I had visited eager to see such ancient graffiti, but resplendent in archaic glory, far from its dead, the church had no soul.

The soul remained, skulking amongst the graves. A puny knight, having lost his armour, ashamed and degraded, mourning the lonely dead ruthlessly left behind. Naked arms, pale-boughed and thorn scraped, caught the corner of my eye twisting into a birch. Ghostly features garish and grotesque watched pitifully from the silver bark as I walked on.

The last proper service was held in 1971. After that, people lit fires on the altar from the scattered pews. A congregation of naked mannequins performed the holy rights to satanism, black magic, sex magic. It was all the rage back then. Some found it funny, others offensive. I thought it expressive, a statement of the times. Frustration, fear and guilt suppressed into outward acts of demonstration, a need to be heard. Not unlike the Passion of Christ hidden beneath its cloak of limewash scorched black by blasphemous fire.

It was here that I found my Aunt Annie's grave. I had forgotten her, until I came home. I remembered Mother saying, don't look at Annie, don't embarrass her, but you couldn't help but stare at the swollen bulging eyelid either side of a purple slit. Never knock on Annie's door if Uncle Jim's car is outside, she'd say, when my friends and I went trick or treating.

I never told anyone about the night I had knocked on their door, my friends scattering when Uncle Jim answered. He'd taken me into the front room and sat me on his knee. A sour stench of whisky mixed with sweat hung about him, I wriggled with displeasure, but it was Uncle Jim, so I had to be polite.

Annie came in wearing a red dress. Her golden hair was up, and she looked really beautiful, except her face was bruised and she kept dabbing at her nose with a tissue. Everyone said I looked just like her and would be just as pretty when I grew up.

Uncle Jim says he's got a treat for me if I'm a good girl, I told Annie, but she began to cry, saying she'd tell my mother if I didn't get home now. I knew I'd have a proper spanking if Mother found out, so I ran. I didn't get any sweets and was upset Aunt Annie had been so mean. I never saw them again.

I was sitting on the wall lost in memories, staring at the old church that wasn't there, watching its soul lament, when a blonde woman in a red coat hurried past. I smiled a hello, remarking on the weather or some such thing. She hesitated then continued her brisk walk towards the river, not looking my way.

A raven barked circling overhead, and a cold wind whipped impatiently. I jumped down from the wall and followed the brown sluggish river. It was then I remembered my mother talking to the neighbour not long after my secret visit. I had only been about seven, but I can recall her words clearly. Poor ole Annie, she'd said. She must have had enough. I hope she's in a better place now, without him. Aye, said the neighbour, shaking her head.

For weeks after I'd asked where Aunt Annie and Uncle Jim had gone and Mother would say she's in a better place now, but not Uncle Jim. Then I grew up and I'm ashamed to say I forgot all about poor ole Annie. The river was silent, the path ahead showing no trace of the blond woman in red. I turned back to the graveyard and the path home, eager to light my log burner.

The raven barked again before descending into a wych elm above a toppled tombstone, lichen patched and mottled. Through the grave bed grey roots gripped the headstone, nudging it aside to claim the rightful place of life birthing from death in the form of wrinkled bark. Twin trunks, limb like, circled each other before joining as one. The waist of the tree rose tall with curved feminine burrs. Boughs unfurled and swayed gently, branches reaching to brush my shoulder.

I traced my fingers over the epitaph still visible through the leafy lichen. Annie, it read, beloved wife and mother. Mother? I thought, touching the cold granite, and then I knew. Looking up into a knotted whorl that twisted and smiled into knowing I began to run, circling the grave.

Author note: I can still hear my own mother's voice say the words, 'Poor ole...' I made up the name Annie, but the story holds an element of truth harking back to the 1970s. The graveyard is very real and can be visited easily along a footpath through the local park in the town of Pontardulais near Swansea, South Wales. The church I also remember as a child being desecrated by would-be satanists, and I remember running around a grave myself seven times but fearing to put my ear to the ground, instead tearing off in fear. Now the ancient building resides in St. Fagan's Natural History Museum and looks truly splendid with its medieval makeover, complete with the uncovered murals. However, the graves remain, overgrown and toppled in the lonely marshland graveyard surrounded by a stone wall where tall wych elms dance in the moonlight.

# Sacks

I didn't take much notice of Ardwyn Cottage before putting in an offer. It was cheap and I wanted something to do up. Structurally it was sound but needed lots of work, so I spent the money she'd paid me off with. She hoped I'd stay as far away from her and my son as I could, to allow her to get on with her new life – complete with new man.

Ardwyn, which is Welsh for *on a hill*, was isolated with only a couple of neighbours dotting the lane. It was the last residence before desolate looking moors yawned and stretched into the black mountains. It didn't appear to sit on the hill so much as crouch, like a gnome spying on the valley below.

Dark grey slates overhung tiny windows, and the walls were so thick they appeared bulbous under dirty flaking lime. Drab green paint peeled from a heavy wooden front door. The whole picture invoked tiredness, the building looked exhausted – not unlike how I felt. I planned to transform it into a cosy pad where my son could visit, whether she liked it or not – I'd see her in court if she tried anything. I envisioned a new lease of life for myself and the cottage.

By the back door, that led into a sizable kitchen dominated by an inglenook fireplace, stood a large rowan tree. I'd never seen a rowan so big. I thought they were wispy things clinging to mountainsides not thick-trunked monsters like this. I didn't think they lived particularly long lives, like oaks, but this one looked unnaturally ancient. The berries were beginning to burst into burnt orange and scarlet, ripening soft and bulging in contrast to the hard grey trunk.

I'd been a builder by trade but the business had gone under during the divorce, so I worked for my mate Dan. He helped me with the renovations on Ardwyn at weekends and before long the cottage breathed an air of cosy chocolate box. I tried to keep things traditional, like the windows and doors; it cost a bit more but I knew people in the trade, so it wasn't too bad. The inglenook was the heart of the kitchen, and I installed a large wood burner complete with oven and hot plate. I saw myself warming soup over a roaring fire after a good moorland walk with my son, muddy boots drying on the old flagstone floor.

The first night I slept there I dreamt a woman was sitting in my bedroom. She may once have been beautiful but was now old and haggard, not like the elderly but like someone who'd suffered. She seemed relieved when I appeared to wake and rushed towards me saying the Divil is dead, God forgive me, the Divil is dead, let him lie. She sighed and dispersed before my eyes. Then I awoke for real and obviously there was nobody there. I tried to get back to sleep but it had left me a little uneasy, so I lay there thinking about my failed marriage until dawn broke my vigil.

I told Dan about the dream the next day, wondering if he knew who the 'divil' may be. He laughed saying it was Irish for devil. That explained it; I'd been listening to The Folk Show on Radio Two that evening. As the late summer sun cooled, I'd sat in the kitchen and lit the fire. Whimsical folksy notes had filled the air mingling with the smell of wood smoke as I ate a simple supper of beans on toast.

The moon had been full and although majestic, resplendent in berries, the rowan tree blocked all light and obscured any view from the kitchen window. I didn't want to contemplate cutting down such a lovely tree, but it was close to the house foundations and may pose a problem. I'd been thinking about this also as I went to bed, with a repeating Irish jig in my head, about the divil no doubt.

That weekend one of the neighbours came by. I felt a little guilty at not having introduced myself sooner, but I'd been so depressed and busy with the cottage and work that socializing was the last thing on my mind. She must have been at least ninety and walked with a stick covered in odd carvings. Sepia skin and lumpy knuckles gripped the knobbly top making it hard to tell where the wood ended and her arm began. Her face, like wrinkled tree bark, broke into a wide gummy smile and a twinkle greeted me from nut brown eyes.

"I see you've done a lovely job of it, bach, 'bout time something was done to brighten the old place up."

"Thanks," I said. "Do you live around here?"

"Yes," she said. "I'm Ivy from the cottage down the lane, Efail-fach – used to be the old smithy – and your nearest neighbour."

"Hello Ivy," I replied, holding out my hand to take her twiggy grasp. "I'm Marcus. Sorry, but I haven't introduced myself to any of the neighbours yet. I hope you'll forgive me."

"You've been much too busy for that by the looks of things," she replied. "But don't worry we'll not hold it against you Marcus, we're a shy lot ourselves but friendly enough."

"Come in for a cup of tea," I said stepping back from the door so she could come into the kitchen. She entered and glanced around smiling as her eyes feasted on the stove complete with kettle on the hotplate.

"That's a good'un," she said. "It'll keep you lovely and snug come winter, and it gets very cold up here."

I smiled at her and proceeded to make tea. I didn't have a tea pot, but she said she could cope with a bag in a mug. I made two builders brews without thinking, but she sipped politely and didn't seem to mind. I asked her about the history of the cottage. It had been a neglected holiday home when I bought it, and neither the vendor nor the estate agent knew much about its past. She sat back in the chair cradling her mug and peered at me over the brim.

"My mam knew the family that lived here when she was just a little girl. I'm over ninety so I'm going back a few years. They were called the Sacks. I can't remember their real name, but everyone called them the Sacks because that's what they wore. They were so poor they couldn't afford proper cloth to make clothes but used old sacking instead. It was tragic really, three little kiddies running around in old sackcloth. My mam remembered the other children at school teasing them, calling them Sacks.

The mother was Irish, worked really hard, but it were him that was the problem. Her husband was a useless old drunk, used to beat her too according to what my mamgu told my mam. She was to stay away from the kids and the cottage just in case; he wasn't to be trusted around little 'uns you see. She told Mam the old rowan tree would have her if she went too close to the cottage." Ivy glanced at the gnarled trunk outside the window and took a tentative sip of tea. It appeared to have heard and loomed closer.

"Is it the same tree?" I asked.

"Oh yes, there's some magic in that old bugger. I've always loved a rowan and that one is older than most. There's a whole lot of daisy wheels carved in the trunk, don't know if they're still visible but you'll see them if you look hard enough."

"What's a daisy wheel?" I asked.

"An old witch mark, guards against evil spirits, a protective charm of sorts. They were very popular years ago; you could find them everywhere. There's a cave in Ireland covered in them, 'twas believed to be graffiti until recently some scholar worked out what they were. My mam said the tree held the devil in it and that's why it had the mark. I wonder what that cave had been holding." She sighed and I almost detected an edge of fear in her voice as she glanced towards the window. "But that's just old wives tales, and rowan trees are lucky trees, protectors of the land," she added hastily, hoping she hadn't frightened me. I suppressed a smile.

"Anyway, the poor old Sacks were starving too, and my mamgu would bring food up for them, she couldn't spare much as times were hard, but she'd give what she could. She took some good cloth up once, to make the kiddies some clothes, but he threw it back at her saying he'd grown up in sackcloth and if it were good enough for him it was good enough for them, nasty bugger. Mamgu reckoned Old Nick himself would have made a better husband." She tutted under her breath, and I thought of the haggard woman from my dream.

"Why didn't she leave him?" I enquired.

"Well, that's the thing you see, she loved him. Said he wasn't always that way, said something had possessed him and she wanted her real husband back. He'd taken her in apparently when he'd been working in Ireland and brought her back to marry her. His family had been poor, but he'd grown up here and it was the only home he knew after his parents died."

Old Ivy took a few more sips of her tea before continuing.

"One day though he disappeared. Nobody knew where he'd gone or what had happened to him. Dead in a ditch some said. Drank himself to death others hoped. Not a single person lifted a finger to look for him; relieved he'd gone they were. My mam didn't realize at the time being only a kiddie herself but the pain and suffering he put his family through was evil. Someone should have done something to help I suppose, but people tended to keep to themselves in them days."

"What happened to her and the kids?" I asked, concerned and hoping for a happy ending now that the wife beating, child molesting drunk who'd clearly taken advantage of a vulnerable woman, had disappeared.

"Well, she up sticks and left, kiddies an all. Dressed in sacks they headed into town looking for work. Maybe she managed to get back to her family in Ireland if she had any but probably ended up in the workhouse or worse. Not many choices for a woman alone with kids in them days. My mamgu gave them some supplies, but she was a proud woman and didn't want charity."

"That's a very sad story," I said placing my cup onto the kitchen counter. The day had begun fresh and clear; now just a corner of sunlight peeped from behind sombre clouds. The rowan cast dark shadows that flitted restlessly around the kitchen.

"Yes," said Ivy. "But at least you're here now and maybe some happiness can return. It's certainly looking like a cosy new home. Is your wife going to be joining you soon?"

Here goes I thought, this was why I had delayed introducing myself to the neighbours. Taking a deep breath, I proceeded to tell her I was divorced, but my son Michael would be visiting, and I was hoping to find some local walks for us to explore. She smiled at this and after telling me to come to hers for a cuppa sometime, she finished her tea and bid me farewell. I couldn't help noticing her give the rowan tree a wide berth.

That afternoon I went for a long walk into the hills and from the top I could see the lane, ribbon-like, winding along the moor and there at the end crouched my cottage. I felt proud because it looked lovely, still gnome like, but one that had had a makeover. Michael would enjoy hiking in the mountains with me. Then I noticed something odd about the rowan tree that was easy to spot with its flame like bundles of berries. A dark shadow hunkered underneath, like someone was hiding and peering through the kitchen window. I wanted to shout out to distract them and let them know I could see them, but I was too far away. I cursed myself for forgetting my binoculars and turned down the hillside hurrying for home, the cottage disappearing from view as I dropped into the valley.

Of course, there was nobody lurking anywhere when I got back, and I began thinking I had imagined it. The sun had been in my eyes, and it could very well have been a black shadow cast from something, although I couldn't think what. I glanced around for footprints in the earth, but the ground was undisturbed.

That night uneasiness rested on my shoulders and although I'd cooked a hearty meal of steak and potatoes with a fresh salad, I had no appetite. The kitchen was cast in shadow and more than once I glanced nervously over my shoulder to the window. I jumped, spilling my beer as I thought I saw a dark shape hunched against the windowsill and was sure I saw the flash of teeth or the white of an eye, but it must have been a cat. I checked outside but saw nothing.

The following morning was a Sunday, and I rose early. I had decided, after a restless sleep dreaming of shadows, daisy wheels and the smell of damp earth and sacking that I would cut the rowan tree down. I phoned Dan and he agreed saying he'd come over to help make sure it didn't fall onto my new roof. I was looking forward to a bit of banter and a couple of beers with him afterwards.

I felt a little guilty about cutting the tree down because it was old, but it wasn't protected, and I promised the land I'd plant some fruit trees to make up for it. I'd always wanted a little orchard. Blossoms would be lovely in the spring, and I may even try my hand at making apple pie. I could do this single dad stuff easily. Michael was going to enjoy his visits.

Coffee mug in hand whilst waiting for Dan to turn up I stood surveying the condemned tree. Sorry mate, I said, but it's time for a change. As I looked closer, I could just about make out a few strange carvings in the bark. There were a couple that looked like a circle with a six-petal flower inside. They were beginning to peel, and I noticed the leaves and berries appeared to have some kind of blight or fungus. Looks like you're already on your way out old boy, I said, touching my hand to the marks on the bark.

A shudder like an electric shock ran up my arm, and a beetle burrowed out of the trunk scuttling away. The tree was being slowly destroyed by the looks of it, which was not a good sign, I thought. It would be a mercy putting it out of its misery, otherwise it would slowly succumb to pests and disease and a strong wind may blow it onto my new roof. I felt better about my decision now. Cutting it down was the sensible thing to do.

Dan and I worked hard and before long the rowan tree was just a pile of logs stacked on the lawn, with its branches and berries arranged in a pyre nearby ready to burn as autumn closed in. We even managed to get most of the root up with a winch. We levelled the ground and prepared it for a patio or maybe a deck, I hadn't decided yet. Feeling pleased with the day's work I lit the barbecue and grilled burgers, which we washed down with a couple of cold beers.

Dan didn't have more than one small bottle as he had to drive home to his family; he'd declined my offer to stay and seemed eager to leave as the evening approached. I envied him watching his truck pull away heading home to all the noise and chaos that comes with family life. I drank the rest of the beers in silence watching the sun sink into the gloaming out of my kitchen window. The walls lit up with a pinkish glow instead of being cast in shadow and feeling satisfied, and a little tipsy, I headed for bed.

I woke up to the stench of damp earth. A heavy weight pressed down on top of me, and I struggled to see through a suffocating blackness. I called out, but rough cloth like sacking pulled tight over my face. As I struggled the cloth tightened, the smell of damp and rot intensified. It's a dream I thought, willing my breath to calm, waiting for the feeling of wakefulness, except I already felt awake. Sack cloth scraped against bare bones and as I tried to move, my mouth fell open to fill with earth.

Fearing choking I panicked, thinking I couldn't breathe – but I wasn't breathing. Stiffened limbs refused to respond like they belonged to some dead thing. Amidst my confusion I sensed a part of me, a lightness that was separated from the bones that gripped like bars, a small frail thing cowering. I reached for it and rose weightless through dying roots and crawling earth only to witness my own body carving a circle with a six-petal flower into a stone. I hung ethereal and formless and saw my lips curve in a cruel arc and mutter strange words that stung my gossamer existence like electric.

Watching helplessly, I saw my own hands place the stone deep in the earth to sit within the withered roots of the poor dead rowan tree, where old bones lay decayed and wrapped in rotten sacking. Something that had never been human stared, laughing at me from behind my own face. Screaming soundlessly my soul plummeted back into the earth and I felt sack cloth pull tight once more over a skull that was not my own. Foreign memories of a woman's frantic cries pressed their way into my being and mingled with children's voices taunting sacks sacks sacks.

Old Ivy had been visiting a friend and was concerned to sense an odd shift in the air when she returned. It felt more significant than simply summer flowing into autumn. The following morning, she smelt smoke and saw a silvery stream meander into the sky. Her new neighbour was having a bonfire by the looks of it. She reached for her stick and decided to take a walk up to Ardwyn to see what he was doing. He had seemed like a nice enough chap. Kind and genuinely concerned when she'd told him about the Sacks, but she'd detected an edge of bitterness when he spoke of his divorce. She hoped this wouldn't make him weak and therefore vulnerable.

Maybe she should tell him about the rowan, how it would be very unwise to chop it down. But how could she tell a story of her mamgu dabbling in witchcraft with the sack woman that resulted in the death of her husband, drunk or not, whilst trying to trap a demon in a tree. If she didn't know better, she'd think it a load of ole cobblers herself. The rowan was old back then and should have been dead by now, but the charms kept it alive, and something still held that foul beast fast. Although she'd had an uncanny feeling Marcus had been thinking about removing the old tree. She hoped the berries would be charming enough to stop him for now, until she'd worked out how to dissuade him without sounding mad.

As she reached the brow of the hill her sharp eyes scanned the view. The outline of the cottage rose defiant and alone against the mountain backdrop aglow with purple heather. Gone was the thick grey trunk and splendor of berries that had dominated the skyline for so long. Her step faltered as fear churned her stomach and she gripped her mamgu's stick, her thumb tracing the sigils carved there long ago, hoping they'd keep her safe.

Marcus was sitting outside sipping from a mug and reading a paper. He looked okay, seemed relaxed even. Maybe it was only an old wives' tale at that, and she was being foolish to think otherwise. The cottage did look better without the crooked old tree leering over it, she supposed. Her eyes flickered to the bonfire where the rowan branches and berries crackled and spat. A young boy stood at a safe distance watching the flames, his son maybe, she thought.

Marcus placed his mug down and looked up at her cautious approach raising a hand in greeting. "Good morning, Ivy," he called, and her heart froze. Icy shards shuddered down her spine oblivious to the morning sunlight as she realised something ancient, something dark and inexplicably evil was smiling at her and recognizing her from behind Marcus's dead grey eyes. She clutched at her chest, and her mamgu's stick clattered to the ground and rolled to rest against the grass verge, the sigils useless.

Author note: The next story came to me after a friend told me a tale her mother had told her, which in turn came from her mother. It was about a family who were so poor they had no money for material to make clothes so instead made clothes from old sack cloth. The locals would refer to them as the Sacks and their true surname was forgotten. The daisy wheel symbol of protection came from legends of how these symbols were carved into stone to ward off evil and offer protection from bad spirits. The rowan tree too, is a symbol of protection against witchcraft and enchantment.

# Where the Bad Wind Blows

It haunts me still. I can feel the chill and hear the bad wind soughing through the few sparse trees that surrounded it. The Wekufe wind the locals said. A soulless bad energy that destroys the natural order. Tomas and some of his Mapuche friends smashed the altar and those awful statues, hopefully breaking whatever spells had been cast there. It was beginning to deteriorate and fold into nature's embrace anyway. It can crumble into nothing and turn to dust for all I care... but I do care, because I can still hear them.

I was living my dream, a trip to Welsh Patagonia. I'd been obsessed with all things Patagonian for many years, the spectacular landscape and wildlife and most of all, my heritage. I am Welsh. I'd traced my family tree back to the Reverend Rhys Dafydd Jones, a distant cousin who in 1865 had set sail from Liverpool with the first Welsh settlers. I was going to follow in his footsteps and be spending two whole months exploring the vast and rugged landscape.

I'd found part time work as a tour guide taking visitors around the sites, like the house of the first settler and leader John Daniel Evans, who was born in Mountain Ash not far from where I grew up. My job involved showing groups of interested parties around the old mill he built, now a museum, and the chapels in and around the quaint village of Trevelin, before finishing off at the rose gardens and tea shop.

It was a pleasant job, and my knowledge of the Welsh language meant I could chat with the visiting Welsh and impress those who had never heard the ancient jumble of letters before. The fact I'd had a cousin who probably knew Mr. Daniel Evans was a bonus. I planned to find out what had happened to the Reverend Rhys, but I'd become distracted spending all my spare time enjoying the adventure tours the Chubut Valley had to offer.

During a hike I'd become friendly with one of the local guides, Tomas. He was Mapuche and a qualified naturalist with a university degree. He was pretty cute too and was with me when I spotted my first Andean puma. Tawny and golden it slunk through the blushing morning mist that rose over rocky mountain crags – a vision to behold, and one I'll never forget… although tarnished now.

Bittersweet memories bring back exciting moments in that glorious wilderness, but shadows rest uneasy on the periphery. I still live in fear that I'll see that dreadful place again. I'd never been afraid of death, always believing in some kind of heaven, but what if there is only darkness… what if that place is all there is? Tomas told me I'm being foolish and maybe he's right, but in the dark when I'm alone I can feel them reaching for me.

I decided to have a break from adventuring and check out the records in the museum to see if I could discover any interesting facts about my cousin. He'd arrived in Patagonia and Trevelin held the last account of him. He'd been responsible for organising the building of a remote chapel. I suppose he believed the homesteads would spread and another village form, but nothing else was out that way. I was hoping to find out what happened to him, but he'd mysteriously disappeared.

The records showed a search party went to look for him. They'd found the chapel, and his cabin abandoned. Whilst there, they were attacked by an indigenous tribe, possibly early Mapuche. The leader spared the men warning them to stay away from that area, saying the Wekufe made the air bad. When questioned they said my cousin had gone to Minchenapu, an evil world lying to the west of Mapu – our world. The search party returned empty handed and the Reverend Rhys Dafydd Jones was marked as missing.

His cabin had long since rotted away so I asked the locals about the chapel he'd built; it was not on the tourist trail and had been largely forgotten. An old lady who made the best Welsh cakes ever to sell in the tea shop, remembered it. She told me it was a strange place where people never went, especially not tourists. She'd messed around there as a kid, a bunch of friends had dared each other to camp, and they'd scared themselves silly. She'd not been back since.

Intrigued, I asked her where this chapel was as I'd like to visit, but she said she didn't know anymore. I pressed her and she became agitated, so I backed off but decided to make it my mission to find this chapel and pay my respects to my distant cousin. I did some digging and found an old map; there was a trail that led out of Trevelin heading into the Andes. There were a few settlements along the way and I spotted a lonely cross. Crosses had been used to mark chapels on old maps, and this was in the area where the search party had been sent.

Tomas confirmed it to be my cousin's chapel and agreed to come with me. I wasn't familiar with the terrain or confident enough to hike alone so I'd need a professional guide. I'd talked him into camping overnight too. I was intrigued as to what had scared the kids all those years ago. Excitement stirred my stomach as the realisation I was going to see something my ancestor had built became a reality. The records were pretty vague about his congregation, stating that only a few settlers had made homesteads out that way, which were now derelict.

The lack of a proper settlement made me wonder what the Mapuche meant about bad air and what was the Wekufe. Tomas told me there were good winds that helped the land prosper and bad winds that brought death and destruction. His grandmother had often spoken of the in between place or Minchenapu where the Wekufe came from, a soulless bad energy. She believed my cousin was a Kalku, a witch, or evil sorcerer. Legend says they dressed in black and commanded the soulless Wekufe to kill and enslave the dead. I told Tomas my cousin would have worn a black robe because he was a reverend not because he was evil.

We passed a few crumbling houses on our way, probably old homesteads. An air of sadness and abandonment draped over their stone shoulders, stooped and decayed. Tomas said there were Patagonian bonneted bats breeding there, not a rare species but good to see nature making use of the old buildings. The path dropped into a valley; Tomas checked the map informing me the chapel wasn't far, and we should be able to see it soon.

Excitement quickened my pace, and I felt connected to my distant relative. Where had he ended up? Had he died of exposure or been eaten by pumas, or both? I hoped he'd gone on to find gold somewhere and lived happily ever after. I didn't even know what he looked like, as there'd been no photographs of him. Did I resemble him? I had green eyes which no one else in my family had. Had his eyes been green too, I wondered.

Tomas stopped and I crashed into his backpack. He pointed upwards to a soaring condor, the body just a black shadow against the cerulean sky, wingtips spread like fingers rippling over air currents. His head, pale and monkish, scanned the valley below. As we watched him glide away my eyes adjusted and down in the shadows I spotted a small stone building. I pointed and Tomas led the way.

I was expecting a tall stark structure built to withstand the elements, hard and authoritative like the Welsh chapels I was used to, but this was small and unnervingly beautiful. It reminded me of a Gothic mausoleum, something an eighteenth-century poet would be buried in not a traditional Welsh chapel at all. It was so out of place nestled in the shadow of rocky outcrops interspersed with dry sand and stone, flushed here and there with sage green. A few shrub-like trees cowered in its presence.

There were two windows either side and one main door in the arched pine end. A strange tower held a heavy stone cross above the entrance where, unlike usual chapels, two stone angels stood guard. Their faces scowled bone coloured and weathered, the features obscured by sulphur-coloured patches of lichen spreading like cancer. I could see why nobody came here; the mask of its initial beauty betrayed an air of the macabre. The door was heavy and surprisingly still intact. Tomas turned an iron ring and shoved it open. A breath of cold silence released into the warm air and the hairs on my neck rose at the cool touch.

Entranced we stepped inside. Shadowed sunbeams penetrated through dirty cobwebbed windows creating a twilight that dappled across two lonely pews arranged before an impressive altar of what looked like black obsidian. The light from the door fell short shrouding it in shadow, where another angel scowled out of the dimness. A faint smell of decay and rot hovered in the stale air that clung to the back of my throat. I looked around for something dead but there was nothing visible. Tomas glanced at the roof but apart from the cobwebs there were no other signs of life.

I sat down on one of the pews oblivious to the dust and tried to picture my cousin preaching to his flock, cloaked in his black reverend's robe. Was he a hellfire and brimstone type, I wondered. By the look of those angels, he probably was. I hoped he'd been a good man, although now I was here, the energy of this place didn't feel particularly joyous. Tomas said he would find a good place to make camp and left me to my musings.

It was odd to feel grief for the death of a distant family member that would have been dead by now anyway. I hadn't even known he'd existed until I'd gone to the library to search my family tree. He'd been a lone name on a dead-end bough, but by chance I'd found the record showing his passage to Patagonia. It was fate; why else had I been obsessed with the place from an early age? It was in my blood and now I was here inside a chapel he had built with his own hands.

A chill brushed my shoulders, and I shuddered. Standing, I approached the altar angel and ran my fingers over the cragged features. A sudden draft made me shiver, and I backed away. Where had they come from? Had he carved them himself? I was beginning to understand why the Mapuche believed him to be a Kalku, a witch or sorcerer. Sighing, I rubbed at a patch of lichen that dragged the stone mouth into a frown. It made his expression worse and left a yellow stain on my thumb which I rubbed into my coat. Poking my tongue out at his worsened grimace I went back into the warmth to help Tomas.

We ate warmed up veggie chilli with our backs to a rock and watched the sun fall into an orange backdrop, the chapel a black silhouette. Tomas said we'd best keep the fire smouldering and take it in turns to sleep, assuring me he never slept much when outside, being fascinated by the nocturnal habits of wildlife. He could survive on very little sleep, he told me confidently, and when he did sleep, he went off immediately and woke at the slightest noise. So, I was not to worry, he'd watch over me.

I'd taken some photos of the chapel with my phone and was flicking through them, making some edits. One caught my eye where shadows fell across the stone angels, giving the impression of flowing robes... or wings. I showed Tomas, who said he didn't like them. He agreed with his grandmother that the chapel was bad; he said he could feel the in-between place, west of the world where evil roamed.

Darkness drenched the valley, and I snuggled into my sleeping bag as Tomas sat watching the fire. I'd say my goodbyes to the long-lost Reverent Rhys's chapel in the morning. Noises of the night echoed over the valley and Tomas identified the lone call of a maned wolf. I fell asleep easily but felt myself weeping. A wind was blowing, and I struggled to catch my breath. A high-pitched wailing lament streamed into my dream, and I woke with a jolt, shocked to feel my sleeping bag and hair drenched with real tears. My heart was hammering, and a tremendous melancholy crushed my usual good spirits.

Sitting up I dried my eyes, quickly glancing at Tomas. He was deeply asleep. I smiled; so much for my nighttime watch. I needed to pee, so pulling on my boots and not moving far from the fire that luckily still smouldered, I squatted worriedly, the fear of insects and snakes never far from my mind when peeing outdoors. On the breeze a sad keening wail pierced the night. Patagonia wildlife can be noisy, but this was coming from inside the chapel.

I should have woken Tomas but my whole body began to crumple as sorrow washed over me. Confused by this sudden reaction I stumbled to the chapel door. My face contorted as sobs wrenched out of my throat, and I pushed into the chapel gloom. The altar emitted an ethereal light casting shadows over the pews, shadows that wailed from eleven heads that turned watching my approach. My own voice keened in return as I entered the congregation. The angel stared accusingly from his plinth of righteousness and willed me to approach, a sulphuric glow seeping from his cancerous features.

Twisted hands reached and clutched. Recoiling I tried to pull away, battling a force that pushed me forwards. My fingers grasped the air dragging my reluctant body to meet the angel's condemning gaze. Shadows flanked, pressing me to my knees as the wailing dirge increased. Bony hands and knotted fingers slid under my hair gripping the back of my neck forcing my face into the obsidian altar. Cold lips brushed the top of my head in an unholy blessing, and I gagged at the sour stench of death.

Through the obsidian an image was forming. Hooded figures writhed and twisted against a woeful wind that blew fiercely over a desolate wasteland. A scream scrambled free of my throat to echo through that land. One of the figures turned knowingly, recognition flashing. Eagerly it rushed to where I knelt at the threshold of that fiendish place of misery and despair. I pressed into my palms to push away from the horror within, but instead of bracing against stone, they fell through to that eldritch place.

Dead hands brushed my fingers, and I stared into the deep hollow face of depression. Skin pulled taught over bone with green eyes weeping regret sought and held my own as I struggled for release. The wailing formed an anguished tune, and I recognised the words to an old Welsh funeral hymn, as one by one the cloaked shadows drifted through to that barren land. A grim wind tugged at my hair, and I too began to fall slowly into the suffering and sorrow, to join the dark congregation of weeping shadows with their wretched reverend.

Another voice drummed on the periphery, Tomas's voice, shouting in his own tongue. It whooshed on the wind of that evil place cutting through my trance and I felt hands grip my shoulders, warm and strong. I fell backwards, away from the terror, away from the wailing and chanting and black robed figures, and into Tomas's arms. We scrabbled on the cold stone floor of the chapel as he struggled to lift me and ran for the door where the glimmer of natural light contrasted with the uncanny glow within.

Tomas grabbed our rucksacks, strapping mine to my back. We left the tents and kicked at the fire to extinguish it. He switched on his torch, and taking my hand we ran from that fearful place. I stumbled and my head unwillingly turned to stare. The chapel door hung open, the eerie light spilling forth, the angels smiling and beckoning, willing my return. Dewch yma fy nghariad, come here my love, the Welsh voice echoed in the air that blew forth. Then Tomas grabbed my hand, and we were running once more.

A feeling of spiralling backwards continued until we left the valley, and the wind dropped. Only then was I able to match Tomas's pace, thankful for his hand that held me fast. We walked through the night, our determined breaths matching the pounding of our boots, until just before dawn we reached his grandmother's house, a small wooden cabin filled with warmth and scented with herbs and spices.

The small Mapuche wise-woman held my eyes as I sat in her fire-lit kitchen drinking hot tea she had brewed, burning my lips on the clay mug. My breaths were ragged and small palpitations fluttered in my chest. She questioned Tomas, her eyes flicking between us, the Mapuche dialect steady, bringing comfort to my fear. Although I understood nothing, I could hear by the tone that I was lucky to be there.

She turned to face me, concern creasing her sage features and sighing she took my hand and stared through my eyes and into my soul. We both knew I'd nearly gone through to Minchenapu, that in-between place where the bad wind blows, and dead things walk. Worshipping misery with hymns of sorrow crying out to the living… where the reverend's eyes are the same green as my own. She dropped my hand with a gasp and clutched at her heart.

"Kalku," were the last words she said.

Author note: Welsh Patagonia fascinates me. It is a place I hope to one day visit, and this story could very well turn into a novel but for the time being it works well as it is. John Daniel Evans, 1862-1943, was born in Mountain Ash in Wales and was one of the early Welsh colonists of Patagonia. The Reverend Rhys Dafydd Jones is a fictional character; his name is simply a mix of popular Welsh names of the time. The early chapels must have looked so stark and out of place in such a wild primal landscape, a juxtaposition to the wilderness and local beliefs and customs of the indigenous people local to the area. *Wekufe* in the Mapuche language means a teller of lies and later became associated with evil and demons. *Minchenmapu* is a place located west of the known world where an evil wind blows and a *kalku* is believed to be a sorcerer or witch that manipulates the *wekufe*. There is so much interesting history and legend surrounding this area that I'm eager to explore and maybe that novel will emerge.

# Through the Yellow Wallpaper

My name is Jane, although I am referred to as the narrator in the story – but then we are all our own narrators. I learned this when I went through the yellow wallpaper.

John meant well, that's what people told me. He is a doctor and should know what he's talking about, but I am a woman and a mother and know far more about my starved soul than he.

At first, I was afraid of her, the woman behind the wallpaper. In fact, I was terrified. She waved frantically, luring me out of bed at night, drawing me towards her and pulling me into that awful colour, but that was its intention. To frighten me away from her. Once I was brave enough to step into it, the hideousness of the colour disappeared.

I almost didn't make it, almost didn't go through. Part of me still doubted the woman and as I hesitated, I heard Jennie knock on the door and peer in. I must have looked a sorry state because I'd drawn blood from my nails tearing at that despicable paper. I watched her eyes open in alarm at my obvious dishevelment. Well, I had been confined for God knows how long in that barred room, which quite frankly was nothing more than a prison cell. Rest cure, they said. A sure ticket to madness more like.

It was this madness I suppose that I feared. I thought the woman was bedlam herself coming to get me. In a way she was, but not how I expected, or John and Jennie for that matter. I knew John would come running, after poor practical doormat Jennie told on me. I'd found a rope too, and had I not gone through the wallpaper I may very well have hanged myself to escape that way.

To buy myself some time, I locked the door and threw the key out of the window. How John hammered and begged to be let in. Fearing he may smash it down before I could get away, I told him the key was outside, probably lying under a plantain leaf by the front door. I heard him scurry away to see if I was telling the truth, giving me a welcome respite to pass into that other place.

Pushing my hands towards the woman in the wallpaper, I braced myself for how she would feel. A wholesome grip took my torn and ragged fingers pulling them towards her and she smiled. Where before she had only been made of shadow, she was now gaining colour, and in that colour, there was beauty. Even the yellow of that damned wallpaper took on a different glow. Like buttercups in a summer meadow.

I pressed my face towards her feeling her hair mingle with my own. I breathed air so fresh that I opened my mouth to taste it. What a difference it was to the stuffy damp-smelling sick room I was leaving behind. As I stepped towards the beautiful smiling woman, who held my hands tightly in her competent grasp, I looked back just as John unlocked the door. How I laughed at his expression of complete bewilderment, as I disappeared into the wallpaper.

I could see his practical thinking mind desperately trying to understand the miracle of what he was seeing, before he fainted. Men deal in facts and science, especially John, he never had time for whimsical fancies or magic, but this was magic of the highest kind. Women's magic, and it was with a laugh and a skip I moved through the yellow wallpaper and into the arms of the woman behind.

For once, in what seemed like an age, I was laughing, and not just a suppressed little smile to show John how timid and well-mannered I was. No. This was truly laughing. Laughing with wanton abandon. The woman laughed too until tears of joy streaked our faces.

Calming myself I observed my saviour. She wore a simple shift of pale yellow that shone in the sunbeams that caressed and danced sensually over our skin. Her feet were bare, as were my own, and I could feel the tender grass between my toes and the scratch of earth on my soles. The woman's hair was brown like my own, but where mine was dull and mousey, hers shone with the radiance of a polished conker.

"Who are you?" I asked, as she smoothed my bleeding fingers. She did not reply except to look into my eyes and pull me into an embrace causing my heart to flutter. Her scent was like wild honeysuckle warmed by the sun, and I returned her embrace burying my face in her hair, wanting to absorb her. Gently she lifted my chin, and I noticed her eyes were forget-me-not blue. I rubbed at my own, grown pale and red and wished to be her.

As if reading my thoughts, she smiled and kissed me full on the lips, before running away like a feral creature through the meadow. I stood transfixed and watched her, this wild and wonderful spirit. My torn fingers rested in wonder on my dry cracked lips, where hers had felt so soft and ripe like cherries. She waved at me to follow as she ran towards the greenwood, dancing and spinning in the summer breeze.

"Wait," I called, as I pulled off my restricting dress and the corset I had been so used to wearing in a bid to prove to John that I was, indeed, a lady. Standing in nothing but my shift I noticed that it too was the prettiest shade of yellow, and like a sunbeam I sprinted after her, feeling like a wild woman myself.

The woods were a temple of green. An air of silence lay over the ancient trees interrupted only by the call of a dove and the whisper of leaves. The earthy odour of leaf mulch and heady resin surrounded us, and my toes sank into a bed of soft emerald moss. Giggling, she took my hands and drew me into her arms, and we tumbled onto the forest floor.

She stroked me, slowly at first, from my brow to my cheeks. Her fingers, light as a feather, followed tendrils of hair as they curled and spiralled across my neck and down my body. My breasts, free from restriction swelled, my nipples hardening to her touch. I gasped as dreamily my eyes closed and I succumbed to her exploration. Shuddering, I felt a tingling reverberating through my most private places and a need so natural I marvelled at its simplicity, awoke inside me.

Spent, I lay like a babe in her arms, drifting off to sleep listening to her voice humming the tune to a jaunty folk song. On waking I reached for her, eager for more of the pleasure she offered, but could feel only myself, touching and probing the parts I had been sworn never to feel. Only John had done so before, clumsily hurting and rubbing. Forcing himself inside me... where a baby had grown.

I could feel the swell of my breasts, and an inner pull where my milk, that had begun to dry up, now began to trickle, dampening my shift. So painful they had been after the birth, needing the suckle of a child, yet my little baby had been given to the wet nurse. Mary, that was her name. She was nursing my child, my little girl.

John had told me she was a good nurse, yet I had heard the little thing crying and crying night after night. I sat up, my fingers digging into the moss and a surge of energy flooded through me, coming from deep within the earth. I must get to my child. The urgency was so great that it caused me to weep like I had wept to John, screaming on my knees when he took her away, assuring me in his practical tones that it was for the best.

I heard a low singing in the trees and entering the clearing came an old woman. Her face was crinkled and dried berry brown, but her eyes twinkled with a thousand galaxies. Long grey hair, wild and matted, hung in dreads over her shoulders, where a silver shawl sparkled with cobwebs. In her hands she carried a large staff, which she used to steady herself and in the other, she held a small leather pouch. At her feet loped a brown hare that flicked its ears to the sound of my cries.

"Ah, I see you have found yourself and awoken the wild spirit within," she said, as a large spider scuttled across her hairline.

"Who are you?" I asked, recoiling in fear. Frantically my eyes scanned the glade for my saviour.

"I have many names. But as for the wild one your eyes search out, she is inside you, my child. She is inside us all."

"Inside?"

"Where she belongs," she said, her voice cawing like a crow as a black robed carrion alighted on her shoulder. Her eyes lingered over my shift, that clung to heavy breasts from which more milk oozed, to run in cream rivulets down my belly and drip onto the earth.

"I need my baby," I blurted. The ancient feeling of motherhood that I had suppressed – believing John that my separation from my child was necessary – began to rise. It beat a primordial rhythm through my blood awakening my heart that thudded against my ribs, and I remembered another, smaller rhythm. The tiny heartbeat I had carried for nine months.

She smiled and laughing replied, "Of course you do, it's natural."

"But how… how can I get her back?"

"I can advise you, but only you can get your baby back. Only you can do that, my dear." The brown hare sat on its haunches and sniffed the air before scratching itself. "It takes strength. Strength you can only get from the wolf within. Now you have released her, you must let her guide you."

With that she sat upon a fallen log, and I watched spiders scurry from the damp wood into her shawl where they began to weave. The hare took his place at her side and the crow cocked his all-knowing stare at me. From her leather pouch she took a handful of bones etched with symbols, which she threw to the ground.

"You are a weaver of tales, a storyteller," she said, studying the fallen bones.

"I like to write, but John – my husband – he said I shouldn't. That ladies do not…"

"Then you have your answer: write your own tale. Be the narrator of your own life."

"But my baby?"

"Yes, your baby will grow up a strong woman by your own example. Take back your story."

A lone wolf howled in the distance, and I noticed the sun had begun to set casting the land in crimson. I saw the path that had led me to the greenwood stretch away across the meadow. The hare began to run towards it before turning to regard me, wise ears twitching.

"Follow the fabled hare out of the wildwood to the fields of civilization," said the old woman and when I looked back, she had gone. Only the crow remained pecking on a dead creature I had not noticed before. The greenwood was darkening as I stepped onto the path to follow the hare.

Soon I had left the wild lands behind, passing my discarded dress and corset, and was standing on the steps to the wretched house John had rented. I looked for the hare only to see a brown shadow dart from view. From inside the cold grey walls, I heard the distant wails of my child. Raised voices greeted me as I entered the hall, and Jennie came hurtling downstairs.

"Call a doctor," she cried before adding, "This is your fault." Her expression was scornful as she regarded me in my simple shift.

I went up to the yellow room and there was John, where I had left him, slumped on the floor.

"Get some smelling salts," I called to Jennie. "It is only a faint; he'll be fine." His eyes opened at the sound of my voice, his faint forgotten.

"Jane," he said scrambling to his feet. "But you… how did you get from inside the walls?"

"Inside the walls? Why John, what is this nonsense you say? I have been out for a walk in the meadow. It is so hot today."

"But I saw you step into that cursed wallpaper, you disappeared!"

The incomprehension on his face was a picture. "John, do be careful dear. There are others here that can bear witness to the onset of madness," I said, smiling at the doctor ascending the stairs. His eyes flickered in alarm to John's distressed form. He had been due to visit and had arrived on time. A doctor of the mind apparently. They were going to discuss my condition.

"I saw her, she walked into the wallpaper!" yelled John. His eyes were bulbous with exertion, as if he could imprint what he saw onto the others that watched him. "Jennie, you were there, you saw."

"No dear John, by the time I returned I saw only an empty room. She must have run outside leaving you where you fainted," said Jennie, glaring at me.

John staggered towards the doctor. "You must believe me," he whimpered, stumbling into my sick room.

"It was here look; she walked straight through the wall. I saw it." He bashed himself into the space on the wall where I had slipped through so easily. The doctor rushed to stop him, but not before John had bruised his head and fists trying to pass into that secret place. He scrabbled at the torn wallpaper, wrenching huge swathes of it down as he searched for a doorway.

"It was here I tell you, here," he yelled. "I saw it. She walked straight through the wall; another woman was holding her hands, pulling her through." He hurled himself into the solid stone once more.

"Quickly, someone help me restrain him, he is damaging himself," cried the doctor as a shocked Jennie hurried to his aid.

I had no time for my husband's madness. I needed my child, whose sobs echoed down the hallway tearing at my senses.

I pushed into the room assigned for Mary to nurse my baby and found only my child alone, crying and calling for her mother. Kneeling at the cot I lifted her tiny frame and placed her at my breast. She latched on to my nipple and hungrily drew the sweet nourishment from within. Wide eyes, forget-me-not blue, stared into my own and a miniature fist clutched and squeezed my thumb.

Mary came running in, flushed and awkward. She had only been gone a few minutes, to empty the chamber pot was her excuse, but I knew she had been out with the stable boy. I could smell the sex on her as she looked at me, shame leaping from her eyes. Slowly her expression turned to wonder as she absorbed what she saw. Jennie bustled in and she too looked at me in awe, speechless for once, as I fed my child, humming the tune to a jaunty folk song.

They could see the transformation in me. They could sense my feral self had awoken, and my wild soul was free. I stood by the window where a spider wove her web, and outside a brown hare loped through the meadow to rest at the foot of an old pedlar woman. She raised her staff in acknowledgement before fading into the greenwood where a crow took flight, its call a loud cackle that lingered in the valley and echoed through the trees.

I smiled, feeling my wild self dance in the sunbeams, and twirl through the buttercups. Laughing and singing I left that house of madness, much to the dismay of those within. I stepped forth to begin a new chapter in my life, powered by the wild one. I cradled my baby girl safely in my arms and walked onto the page of a new story… a tale where I would be the narrator.

Author note: 'Through the Yellow Wallpaper' is simply that: a journey through to save the woman trapped within. It is a rewrite of the dark psychological novella 'The Yellow Wallpaper,' a semiauto-biographical story written by Charlotte Perkins Gilman published in 1892. She wrote it after suffering severely from post-partum depression. I felt I needed to write a positive outcome to turn the tale around and release the woman from her madness.

# Whispering Poplars

*Panic washes through me as I watch the roots and vines shift and mummer; like tubes they feed and probe carrying nutrients. My head swims, my mind is whirling, and I can't feel my body – it's as if I am everywhere yet nowhere. There is heat rising, burning from below to burst forth above and through it all I can hear a voice, her voice laughing. Other voices join and soft music plays like tinkling bells and thrumming vibrations, relaxing me even though I do not want to relax. Spell-like it subdues me, and I feel something, a quickening inside, another life within.*

\*

The house had sat empty for years, in fact no one can remember a time when it had last been lived in. It was called Whispering Poplars, because it languished within a circle of poplar trees that guarded and whispered in the breeze. Local kids referred to it as the haunted house, and their parents did too, remembering the empty shell when they were young, and their parents before them. I was not local, I was just passing through and decided to stay for a while, and I'd been squatting in the old house for about a week now.

Legend spoke of a white lady that danced through the rooms, twirling long skirts, and strange music that floated through the windows on warm summer nights. There were tales of faeries and people going missing for a hundred years to return unchanged, but these were stories that abounded on this island. I'd not seen any white ladies or heard any music although there was an eerie feel to the place. I was just happy for a dry floor and a roof over my head. Fairies and dancing ladies were welcome as long as they didn't report me for illegal squatting.

The local library had no more information about the enigmatic house, apart from a description of its somewhat uncanny neo-Gothic architecture, having bizarrely modern influences hidden beneath a parody of Gothic styles, and of course the White Lady legend. Although weathered, I had noticed the creamy stone appeared oddly metallic in the sun giving the many gargoyles that lay watch upon the hooded moulds above the windows and large porch a strangely golden sheen. The old windows were intact with not a smashed pane in sight, and unlike some empty houses no old furniture sat rotting inside either.

I was having breakfast in the village cafe and enquiring about work – my funds were running low. The waitress told me there was always work pot washing in the kitchen, both at the cafe and the local pub. She said she'd sort something for me. We got talking, and she was intrigued as to why a young woman like me was living this kind of vagrant life. I didn't go into the gory details of my abusive father and dead mother but told her I'd always been a traveller at heart and liked life on the road under the stars. I was free this way and answered to nobody.

We became friends of a sort, over the week I'd been there, and I accepted when she asked me to go with her to the pub that night. I didn't usually socialize but I liked her company and to be honest I felt like a laugh and a few drinks. She called herself Ari, short for Arianrhod. I hesitated to give my own name, as I always made one up, but this time I decided to tell her my birth name – Stella.

"Stella?" she enquired to which I nodded. "What a beautiful name," she said, staring as if she'd only just noticed me.

"Arianrhod is a pretty name too," I remarked.

"It's an old name," she said, green eyes regarding me seriously before smiling and exclaiming, "In fact, it's so old it's practically medieval." She laughed and I joined in. "But Stella means star, do you like stargazing?" she asked more seriously.

"Yes I do, and when I was a kid, I used to love sleeping outside just to gaze up at the constellations."

"Do you know Cassiopeia? It sits brightly in the sky above the old poplar house. Even when you can barely see it elsewhere, it's still visible there. The Celts called it the circle of Don."

"Who's Don?" I asked.

"The Welsh mother goddess. Giver of life to all. My

Mother's name is Don too, short for Donia, it's pretty don't you think?"

I had to agree it was a pretty name. I thought back to my first night at the poplar house, and she was right, the whole of the night sky seemed more vivid from that place. The Milky Way like a celestial snake lounged across the darkness with Cassiopeia shining brightly across its abdomen.

"Does your mother live in the village too?" I asked.

"No, she keeps her distance. It's far too boring for her."

The village was on the verge of becoming a market town but still held on to a dismal version of rural charm. It had some tourists, but being away from the coast with not much historical or natural beauty nearby, it hadn't really flourished. It seemed to be relatively self-sufficient though, with a healthy high street and the villagers didn't appear to want for much.

"Do you have any brothers or sisters here?" I wanted to learn more about this beautiful, charming girl.

"Some, but they've moved away. Mother can't have children very easily, even though she wants them – but it doesn't stop her trying."

"Like fertility treatment?" I asked.

"Something like that," she answered wistfully.

I wasn't quite sure what she meant and decided not to press further knowing all too well what dysfunctional families were like.

The local pub did basic food, with a restaurant area that had a proper chef on Saturdays and Sundays only. True to her word Ari got me a job as pot washer at weekends. The land lady hadn't wanted to know where I lived so the knowledge of my squatting in the haunted house was still a secret. I was thankful to Ari for not telling anyone. We sat at a small table just off the bar and she treated me to a supper of scampi and chips.

"So, what's it like sleeping in that old place?" she asked, drenching her chips in vinegar and popping one into her mouth, smiling as she chewed adding, "God, these chips are good."

I hesitated in my reply shrugging my shoulders before

pulling an ecstatic expression, as I too stuffed my mouth with hot greasy chips smothered in salt and vinegar.

"Do you get scared all alone?" she ventured.

"Well, I suppose sometimes," I replied, wiping my hands on the paper napkin. "But I'm used to it, and I've slept in worse places."

"Aren't you afraid of ghosts?" she asked through a mouthful of chips.

I laughed a response, "It's the living that hurt you not the dead, and I'm not sure I believe in ghosts or spirits, or anything supernatural."

"But haven't you felt or heard anything?" She leaned towards me holding my eye.

"Not really," I lied. "I sleep too soundly for that."

I'd had a few nervous nights at the house, which I wasn't going to reveal, just strange sounds and dreams. A soft thrumming seemed to vibrate through the rooms, and I'd feel like I was floating, and begin to panic but then I'd wake up needing to pee. I'd go outside and watch the poplars sighing in the night breeze and try not to feel self-conscious about the gargoyles watching me empty my bladder. I often had bad dreams, some worse than others, but these usually reflected a past I wished to forget.

As for the sounds, well nature can be a noisy companion when there's no double glazing between you and poplar trees, renowned for whispering leaves, although I'd not noticed much wildlife near the house and the chants and warbles of songbirds sounded distant. None appeared to roost or nest in the surrounding poplars or even in the eaves of the roof or chimneys, which I found odd.

"Shall we hold a séance there tonight, see if there's any truth to the haunted rumours?"

"A what?" I felt a little uncertain.

"You know, like the Ouija board."

"I know what it is. I'm just not into that sort of thing."

"I thought you weren't scared?" She reached for my hand across the table. My breath caught and I moved, but not before allowing our fingers to touch. I suppose she had enchanted me with her golden curls, curious green eyes and soft creamy complexion. I felt dull in comparison with my dark straight hair, lank and unwashed, and skin tanned from walking the roads.

I reluctantly agreed to the séance, and it was lovely to watch Ari jump about all bubbly and excited, even pecking me on the cheek. When we finished our meal and drinks, she paid for mine too. I told her I'd pay her back after my first weekend of pot washing, but she just dismissed it as not important. Leaning over the bar she shouted a cheery goodbye to the landlady, who was deep in conversation at the other end, and stole a pile of beer mats and a glass. Winking at me she slipped them into her bag, and we began the walk out of the village towards Whispering Poplars.

Midge flies hummed in the warm air, and I got stung a few times but noticed they didn't seem to bother Ari even though her pale complexion would usually attract them. The moon was a gentle sickle hanging lazily in a starlit kaleidoscope. The beers I'd drunk had left me contented and I hoped Ari had forgotten all about having a séance. I knew she was flirting with me, and I was interested in her too. I'd not been close to anyone for some time now.

The poplar trees came into view first, a slight draft stirring the leaves causing them to quiver and mutter at our arrival. Ari swirled, spreading her arms wide and reached up to the first tree picking a leaf.

"Can you see where the leaves have been singed, by fire?" she said showing me the darker surface in comparison to the paler underside.

"Was there a fire here then?" I glanced around at the lack of ash or burnt debris.

"Not here silly," she giggled. "The poplar tree is said to guard the underworld. The realm of Hades, the fires of hell if you're religious, or the land of faerie if you believe the ancient Celts."

I smiled, thinking she looked particularly nymph like skipping up the path to the old house that watched our approach through empty windows.

"Do you think hell lies beneath or above, far away in deepest space?" she asked, gazing at the sky which was particularly dazzling. "Or fairyland, as I prefer to call it," she said.

"Well, I've not given much thought to hell or fairyland, or heaven for that matter," I replied, aware that the conversation was going over my head a bit. I looked behind us; the feeling of being observed was heightened, and the constant whispering from the trees was beginning to sound like white noise, or the gentle purring of an engine. As we passed under the arched porch, I noticed one of the gargoyles looking directly at me, the head angled quizzically on a scaled body. I hadn't really studied it before but the metallic sheen to the stonework was very noticeable at night, illuminated by starlight.

"The stonework looks weirdly shiny at night, don't you think?" said Ari.

"Yes, it must be an optical illusion with the light or something," I replied.

"Like a spaceship waiting to whisk you away," she giggled. "The gargoyles guardian robots."

"You've watched too much Dr. Who," I said as she spun in a circle with arms outstretched. "Anyway, why has this place been empty for so long? It's in pretty good shape. Surely some rich investor would have snapped it up?" I asked.

Ari stopped spinning and regarded me as if I was stupid. "Because it's haunted, silly," she replied, matter of fact. I noted that was the second time she'd called me silly. Was I really being silly I wondered, watching her dainty feet skip up the steps to the heavy wooden door. With a flourish, she lifted the old bronze knocker that resembled a satyr with face and horns leering out of a circle of intricately layered leaves, like a wicked Green Man. Seconds hesitated as the knocker hovered suspended, before falling against the wood and a boom reverberated through the empty rooms.

"Don't be so dramatic," I said breaking the spell and pushing through the doorway. She followed, closing the heavy door behind. I heard it shudder with an ominous crack as the catch caught, crunching it shut.

Ari noted my humble camp in the living room. I felt confident enough to leave my stuff out as if I lived here, something I rarely did in other places. I'd made it cosy. I got my lighter and lit the portable oil lamp I carried and the small gas stove.

"Tea or coffee?"

"Oh, coffee please," purred Ari. "This looks really sweet; you've got everything you need." She eyed my supplies, and the small washing line I'd strung up to dry a few clothes I'd managed to wash in the village launderette and couldn't afford to tumble dry.

As I busied myself with making the coffee and lighting a few candles I always carried, Ari began writing the alphabet onto the back of the cardboard beer mats, and on the last two she wrote a large YES and NO. She placed them in a circle on the floor with the stolen glass in the middle and we both sat on my bed roll sipping coffee from the same mug, as I only had the one. Her writing was swirly and decorative, skilful and calligraphic, making the common beer mats look artistic and antiquated.

"So, we're really doing this?" I asked.

"Yes," she said, kneeling before the circle and indicating for me to do the same. "Place your finger very lightly on the glass and close your eyes. If you feel it move, you can open them."

I felt a bit foolish and hoped nothing would happen because I had to sleep here after all, and I didn't fancy moving on just yet. Ari's voice echoed around the empty room chanting the usual lines for attracting the ghostly dead to communicate through the glass. I opened my eyes to watch her and was surprised to see how serious she'd become. Her head was thrown back, her voice monotonous and repetitive. I suppressed a giggle as she began muttering in a language I didn't recognise.

"Are you making these words up, Ari?" I whispered.

"Ari," I said more seriously, "it's not working."

She didn't respond and looked as if she hadn't heard me. Fear raised my neck hairs, and I was about to tell her to stop when the glass began to judder.

It moved to YES, before beginning to slowly circle the alphabet. I looked at Ari shocked, because I hadn't moved it, but her eyes had rolled back like she was in some kind of trance.

"Ari! Ari look at me," I cried, taking my finger off the glass and taking her hand in mine, I rubbed it briskly. When that didn't work, I shook her by the shoulders. I was worried she was having a fit or something. I brushed her hair off her face telling her to stop messing around as it wasn't funny anymore. Her eyes flickered, the pupils realigning like fruits in a slot machine, and she regarded me slowly beginning to laugh. I wanted to slap her for teasing, except something felt off, it didn't sound like her voice; it was distorted and robotic, stuttering like a bad recording. I backed away.

"It's not funny Ari, you're scaring me. Stop it. Stop laughing. How are you doing that?"

I indicated the glass that was continuing to circle the letters even though neither of us had our fingers in place. The glass scraped on the wooden floor getting faster, the sound making my teeth tingle. The whole room began to vibrate, and I ran for the door. Swinging it open, a gargoyle head swivelled in my direction and a body encased with plates of gold armour rose on hind legs. Eyelids blinked over black holes holding spinning lights and I saw my own terrified face captured like a photograph before they blinked again. Suction noises and gasses burst from the joints as it moved agilely to block my escape, but on seeing the outside I slowly backed into the hall.

Fires dotted a twilit landscape as the poplar trees spun, their branches waving like crazed dancers, the noise a frantic rushing. The driveway and distant village were nowhere to be seen. I felt the house begin to lift; it rose in a steady rotation to hover delicately above the now blurred landscape. I raised my arms to protect myself from the white almost blinding heat that burned from beneath. The door knocker began to laugh and jabber, the words a torrent of nonsense, whilst the leaves circling the satyr's face spun like the trees. The gargoyle retook his place as sentinel under the porch and the door slammed shut.

I turned to Ari as the room transformed. My cosy corner was being consumed by creeping roots and vines sprouting from the floors, and a bulbous membrane enveloped the walls that began to pulse with a strangely beautiful pearlescent lilac and green. Ari was standing draped in white, and saint-like she reached for me. The beer mats were swirling around her like fallen leaves whipped by an invisible wind, the alphabet flashing past. The glass too continued its circling, rising higher before smashing to the floor. Ari hovered spirit-like, her head cocked at an angle querying my reaction, a half-smile curling her lips.

"Mother and Father welcome you Stella," was all she said. I ran for the door that led to the rest of the house hoping to see the empty rooms and the world as I knew it outside, but everywhere I ran had transformed into the soft bulbous tissue interwoven with the throbbing, pulsing roots and vines, emanating a now phosphorus glow. I had no idea what they were, except they moved and breathed as if alive. A steady thrum was vibrating, lifting and descending, palpitating in my heart to hold rhythm with the blood pumping adrenalin rich through my veins. The tissue encasing the walls and floor was silky and pillow-like, and I felt as if I was trying to run across a billowy mattress. I'm dreaming I thought, this is just a dream, but her voice cut through.

"Do not fight it Stella, succumb to Father and allow him to hold you and let yourself fall into Mother." I struggled not to, but fall I did, my face pressing into the soft silkiness. The thrumming increased, the same sound I'd heard in my sleep previously and had dismissed as the breeze whispering in the trees. I felt like I was being carried on a cloud spiralling through the night sky. My limbs began to stiffen, as my tired muscles gave up their fight. I sank into the softness and my eyes searched for Ari. She reached for me; her willowy form flickered once and went out leaving me alone in the darkness, and I succumbed.

Voices trickled over my helpless form as I languished in a dream state, neither awake nor asleep. Unable to move. I wasn't even sure I was breathing as no breath entered or left my lungs. Slowly I felt the dark roots and green vines tangle through my limbs touching parts of my body, tingling and awakening senses, gently probing and searching. My consciousness detached and I was able to look down at a misshapen form twisted and broken, writhing and thrashing. Blood flowed crimson through translucent veins feeding and centring on a pulsating mass low down in the abdomen – my abdomen.

The vines held my limbs, and I saw the roots had torn through my body invading it, brutalizing it far worse than my own father had ever done. My mind hung like a spark of brilliant light, terrified of what was revealed to it below – terrified of the body. My body, that fed the unborn child curled pulsing and shimmering beneath greying diaphanous skin entwined in roots and vines – or were they wires and tubes?

Whispers and murmurings floated on air currents as soft music played, and gossamer figures danced, circling in a twilit sky against the backdrop of five glowing orbs, spread out like Cassiopeia, close enough to touch. A hazy cluster of stars twisted into a spiral leading down like a staircase, to a tiny blue and green planet, whilst all around leaves fell like ash.

Author note: Poplar trees whisper in the breeze, and their leaves are dark on top and pale underneath as if they have been burned. They are also believed to grow at the entrance to the realm of the dead, the Underworld, and are sacred to Hades. There is much information about Arianrhod the Celtic deity, a goddess of fertility, rebirth and the interweaving of cosmic time and fate. A goddess of the moon and stars who lives in a revolving castle in the sky called Caer Sidi, according to some sources. She is the daughter of the mother goddess Don in Welsh folklore, whose name translates to 'silver wheel.' The constellation of Cassiopeia's Chair is known in Welsh tradition to be the Circle of Don, and the Northern Crown is the circle of Arianrhod. What if the land of faerie existed in these distant constellations and an old mansion could also be a spaceship or a revolving castle that can travel between the worlds? But what of the fair folk? Would they be just as wicked as legend suggests?

# Why Don't You Turn Around and Look at Me?

I found myself walking the wild sandy expanse of Rhossili Bay, one of my favourite places in the world. I always come here when things get challenging. Or if I'm visiting my old home in Swansea, this is where you'll find me. The familiar rocky outcrop and landmark known as Worm's Head rears ancient and menacing out of the water. A spray of gulls spewing from its stone mouth spreads across the mackerel sky.

I decided to sit for a while, alone with the *Helvetia*, a half-buried Norwegian wooden shipwreck dating from 1887. It cradled me within, what had once appeared as a shattered ribcage, but over the years the tide destroyed the remains. Covering it with sand, leaving nothing more than a few jutting pieces of wood. The ribcage simply an embellished memory from my past. The ship had been lured to the treacherous rocks by smugglers, with their false lanterns, a gruesome history this coastline was famous for.

I gazed up at the shore and contemplated the reasons for my recent return home. The empty rectory that overlooked the bay stared back with lidless windows, silent and reproachful. Some said it was haunted by a being that crawled out of the sea. A demon that challenged you with a cold hand on your shoulder to turn round and look at it – something you should never do. I'd read about it in a book on Welsh legends as a child and it frightened me.

My recent accident frightened me too. I still couldn't remember much, it felt vague and a bit mystifying, obviously caused by the head injury I'd sustained – which ached. I was still disoriented and confused and couldn't recall how I had arrived here, back at Worm's Head, but here I was. Had my accident happened nearby maybe? Or I probably just gravitated here when I felt unwell.

A tangle of oystercatchers and gulls screeched from the shoreline as I stood to continue my walk, a circular through the dunes along the beach, then a picnic at the top to admire the view, and back over the mountain. I felt for my backpack and was relieved to find it stocked with goodies: water and a flask of coffee. Another action I'd obviously done and forgotten about. I wondered if I should even be out on my own.

Steps ascended steeply to the grassy cliff top dotted with sheep and wild ponies. I began the laborious climb, stopping only briefly to admire a hovering kestrel, that was quite unaware of my presence so engrossed was he in the tiny rodents below. I felt pleased with myself, as I was hardly out of breath, the steep incline being no easy task. I must be recuperating well, I thought.

At the top my usual seat was occupied by a rather ragged fellow. I gave him a cheery hello, but he ignored me. He was concentrating on something out to sea. I followed his line of vision but couldn't make out what he was looking at. Feeling a little uneasy I decided to walk towards Saint Mary's Church, and there enjoy my picnic in the graveyard overlooking the bay. It's a quiet churchyard with a spectacular view across to the old rectory and the curving bay.

I noted for the first time that my clothes were wet. I tried to recall if I had paddled in the sea and been splashed by waves, or was it when I sat on the sand by the *Helvetia*? Maybe my sensory awareness had also been disrupted due to the head injury, and I'd sat in a puddle without realising. But I was terribly wet, almost as if I had been swimming with my clothes on.

I tucked into my sandwiches and glanced around at the headstones. A stench of morbid realisation arose as I began to imagine the bodies lying beneath my feet. Were they still in coffins? Or had the wood rotted, exposing the earthly remains dressed in Sunday best to be feasted upon by a myriad of insects and worms, the corpses newly animated in a dance macabre of wriggling scurrying masses as the bones were stripped bare.

I spotted the ragged man I'd seen earlier, by the graveyard wall; he was watching a little girl I'd not noticed before. She was dressed almost as raggedly as him, and I was becoming concerned as to where her parents might be when I saw a woman walking my way. Glancing briefly at me she gave a curt nod before sitting down on the same bench. I felt a little foolish with my picnic paraphernalia spread about, almost like a little boy, and I hastened to tidy them up before offering her some coffee.

"No thank you," she replied, so I continued to pour myself a cup from my flask.

"Who's that unsavoury fellow over by the wall?" I enquired as I sipped from my childhood mug, wondering where I had found it after all these years. Mother had bought it for my boy scout camping trips, it was enamel, and I had imagined myself a brave explorer when drinking from it.

She sighed as if tired of a familiar conversation, before saying, "He is the girl's father, although he's not allowed near her now."

"What do you mean?" I asked, glancing nervously over my shoulder at the man who had now focused his attention on us.

"Don't worry, he knows he can't come into the graveyard," she replied with a sigh.

"Is she safe playing so close to him? Are you her guardian?" I enquired, noting her rather old-fashioned appearance, long skirts and dark hair pinned up; maybe she was a governess or something. Did they still have them or were they called child minders these days? But maybe children's homes had a more traditional approach ...

"I suppose I am, but there are others." She beckoned to the little girl who came over to sit cross legged on the edge of a tomb next to us.

"Hello," I said. "Would you like a Welsh cake?" I noticed I had a packet of the perfect little cakes my mother used to bake, full of currants and sultanas. She smiled and took one gingerly from the package. "Take them all," I said, as beaming she took the rest and skipping away, made a little picnic of her own in a patch of yellow primroses.

"What happened?" I asked quietly, nodding in the direction of her father who had returned to his seashore vigil. There was a dark shape on the beach he was watching intensely. I couldn't quite make out what it was.

"It was to do with the smuggling; she refused to carry the light to lure the ships and instead tried to help the drowning. She'd had enough of death."

"What do you mean, smuggling? Do you mean drugs?"

She shrugged, and there came that tiresome sigh again. "Anyway, she paid for her disobedience with her life, as did the poor sailors she tried to help."

"What?" I glanced towards the little girl who seemed very much alive, smiling and munching on my mother's Welsh cakes with primroses in her hair. Then I realised, they couldn't be my mother's Welsh cakes because she had been dead for over ten years.

"Her father threw her off the head of the Worm," said my companion.

"What?" I exclaimed, looking over at the infamous rocky outcrop. The wind had picked up, clouds were gathering, and the sea roiled to crash and spray over the cliffs. The dark shape had dragged itself further up the beach. "How did she survive?" I asked, confusion eddying on the shores of my mind.

"Look," she said suddenly. "It will come for you, it always comes for those that have links to the Worm, and you need to resist it. Don't look at it when it asks you to." She proceeded to wring her hands before adding, "My husband failed, I will never see him again, it consumed him, and he is lost to me. He could have returned, had he not looked…"

"What are you talking about?" I said, aware that I was the one with a head injury, yet she was the one talking a load of nonsense.

"You remind me of my husband," she said, her face brightening. The previous conversation was already dissipating from my mind, and I couldn't think why I had become a little alarmed. "It's the mug," she said, indicating my enamel coffee cup that rested on my knee, my fingers curled lightly through the handle. "He had one just like it which he used to take on expeditions."

"What sort of expeditions?" My interest piqued.

"Oh, he went on many adventures." Her eyes took on a dreamy haze, her mouth tweaking in a private smile, a coy little trait meant only for him, making me feel like I had intruded on her innermost thoughts. "In fact, he was quite famous," she added, turning her head away to hide the tears that brushed her cheeks.

I got the idea from her use of the past tense that he was probably not alive anymore and I was intrigued to know who this great adventurer was, yet I didn't want to upset her.

"His name was Edgar Evans," she said.

The name certainly rang a bell. There was a memorial to him inside the very church whose graveyard we were sitting within. A dreamy stained-glass window depicted the cold blue glow of an icy far away wilderness, because *that* Edgar Evans had been aboard the *Terra Nova* bound for Antarctica in 1911. The whole party had come into problems during the arduous trek back from the South Pole. Edgar Evans had fallen during the expedition, incurring a nasty head injury. He died on February 17th, 1912.

Some say he must have experienced insanity at the end, and it would not have been an easy death. He was the largest of the men and took equal rations, even though he likely did most of the sledge pulling. His comrades had died soon after, none of them ever reaching the *Terra Nova* again. Probably, because of his Welsh working-class background, he was fair game to the press and initially blamed for the failure of the whole expedition. His wife Lois, who he'd grown up with, was also hounded by the press. She fought hard to restore his reputation and was responsible for the plaque inside the church.

"Edgar Evans?" I questioned. I wanted to ask if he was related to *that* Edgar Evans, maybe he was his grandson or something. "I'm sorry for your loss," I said instead. I was getting confused again as a result of my own recent head injury, which had begun to throb once more. I still had some sandwiches laid out upon the wall; I thought I had finished them. "Would you like a cheese and pickle sandwich?" I asked.

She smiled and stood up briskly. "Look, I should go." She

glanced nervously towards the bay; the sky had darkened considerably, and a storm was lurking on the horizon. The bright sunlight of the afternoon almost entirely swallowed by what was brewing out to sea. I cursed my stupidity. I still had a long walk left to reach the car, unless I had parked it next to the church, but why couldn't I remember? I rubbed my eyes as if that would give my fuzzy mind some clarity.

"It's been lovely chatting with you," I said, getting to my feet. I seemed to have already packed my things into my backpack and was fit to go. I glanced around for the little girl to say my farewells, but she had disappeared. Her ragged father had returned to his bench overlooking the sea and was studying the dark shape that had reached the steps. I was relieved I wouldn't need to pass his way again, when I realised, I didn't know the name of my companion and I hadn't introduced myself either.

As if reading my thoughts she held out her hand saying, "I'm Lois. Lois Evans." My fingers brushed against hers and she snatched her hand away before I could properly take it.

"I'm Idris," I said. "Idris Williams."

"Try to resist it Idris," she said. "It will try to take you and next time you may not be strong enough to make it back here."

"Whatever do you mean?" I asked, aware that I may be missing some vital piece of information which my mind was unable to process.

"It's the demon," she said. "It will come for you, and you must not look at it or you will never find peace."

"But I don't believe in such things. Is this something to do with that silly tale about the rectory?" I exclaimed, not wanting to remember my childhood fear.

"It's not just the rectory. It searches for souls that wander the shadows to reach the place they once held such love for. The Worm," she said, looking out at the rocky dragon. "It comes for the lost and the dying. You must not look at it."

"Please, I'm sorry, I have enjoyed our chat, but all this talk of demons is a little unnerving. It's just an old legend, a ghost story, not anything real, now please excuse me," I blustered. "I've got a long walk ahead and this storm looks almost upon us… and I'm not lost or… dying," I added, rubbing at my aching head, but she'd already hurried away disappearing behind the church.

I followed the path around the side of the graveyard and on towards the little car park, hoping to see a familiar vehicle, although I couldn't quite recall what car I drove these days. As I neared the wall I saw the ragged old man again. He looked like he wanted to say something, so I quickened my pace, but he beat me to the gate.

"It's coming," he said, "and you won't be able to resist. You may make it back, but this is your third time now. You're getting more and more forgetful."

"Shut up," I said trying to push past him. I didn't know what he meant by third time. This was my favourite place, I'd been here hundreds of times.

"Next time you'll be well and truly lost and it'll consume you, and you'll never find peace – only darkness." He spat the word darkness, and I recoiled.

"Please, let me pass or I'm going to report you to the police."

"Report me? Don't make me laugh, nah, you'll not make it this time, mark my words. I've seen it happen," he cackled. The sound blended with a clattering of jackdaws that took off from the church roof and swirled over the rectory.

"Leave me alone," I cried. "I heard what you did to that little girl, your own daughter too. What kind of monster are you?"

"Monster, you think I'm a monster? Just you wait and see." He looked behind me and I watched his face twist into fear, and he began to step backwards. His ancient, scuffed boots scraped the path, tripping over each other.

I felt something at my back and watched a shadow cast its length before me, as the last of the sunlight vanished into the broiling mass of cloud. My muscles were stiff and chilled under my wet clothes, and I gave an involuntary shiver. A cold hand touched my shoulder, and a sibilant voice hissed close to my ear. "Why don't you turn round and look at me?" My temper at the ragged man, who had now turned and fled, flared, and before I could heed the warning poor Lois had given, I swung round.

The sea is freezing, and I can't reach the shore. My head hurts and I can't feel my limbs, but I can sense a presence nearby and it frightens me. I don't know what it wants but it keeps tugging at my thoughts or is that the sea pulling me under? It will not relent. I try to remember what I had been doing, and then I see my kayak capsized and broken on the rocks.

I'm afraid, scared of the dark that is fast approaching. Dusk is rapidly turning to night, and I keep my eyes peeled on the deep lilac skyline, some desperate inner will to survive telling me to do so. Then I see a beacon. A tiny light flashes against the rock just below the rearing head of the mighty Worm. Spume from the sea batters against it, spraying forth like dragon's breath.

There's a little girl dressed in raggedy clothes, beckoning, she's gesturing frantically. Recognition flickers through the fog. I had a picnic in the graveyard of Saint Mary's church, was she there? Did I give her a packet of my mother's homemade Welsh cakes? Yes, she had sat smiling amongst the tombs, crumbs on her face and yellow primroses in her hair. She didn't want to take the light, I recall, but instead had tried to help the drowning.

I force my arms to move and swim towards the little girl, frantically pushing against the sea. A shadow rises behind her haloed form, and I recognise the ragged man. I know what is about to happen but am too far away. I cry out in warning but watch helpless as the light bobs, falling to the rocks below where it smashes into the night, and a screech of gulls rise from the cliffs.

Thrashing in the water I struggle to get to the rocks, to reach the shore. I remember where the lantern was, where the little girl lies broken. My head throbs, the cold water is numbing, and I feel myself falling into darkness. Spiralling down. I fight it but I am being swallowed, consumed by the depths. I realise what Lois meant now. I must be dead. I missed my chance of redemption.

A vision of Rhossili Bay on a summer's day flickers in my mind and a childhood fear rears its demonic head – a warning not to look. I want to return. Get back to the little church, to try again and resist the urge to turn around – to not look at it. I curse my ignorance, and the ragged man who distracted me. Murderer of the little girl, known only in the smuggling legends I'd read as a child.

Did Edgar Evans hear the same voice? Did he succumb to the sibilant hissing far away as he lay in frostbitten madness stranded in Antarctica? His spirit never to return to this place, never to thank his wife for her enduring love? Am I to be lost forever too, drowned by the gaze of a demon I failed to resist? My soul to know only darkness, extinguished and swallowed by the mighty Worm? A Worm that lies ancient and menacing, its outline stark and legendary against the night sky.

Author note: A good friend found an old tatty book on Welsh smuggling legends in a charity shop. Inside was a story of how a young girl, feeling for the souls of the shipwrecked, refused to carry the lamp. Carrying the lamp was what people did to lure the ships onto the rocks to then steal the cargo. Legend says she was pushed, by either her father or the other men of the village, off the end of Worm's Head where she fell to her death at Rhossili beach in Wales. I also found a book of Welsh legends where I read a terrifying story about something that crawls out of the sea to place a hand on your shoulder and hiss, 'Why don't you turn round and look at me?' Even saying those words sends shivers down my spine. The little church of Saint Mary on the headland however, is a haven of peace and tranquillity where you can enjoy the cool, icy colours of Anne Clarkson's stained-glass window dedicated to Petty Officer Edgar Evans.

# Heart and Home

Every day without fail she would put on her cotton apron and perform her chores. Religiously. Whole days were put aside for polishing the hardwood floors, dusting the cornicing, scrubbing the fireplaces. Not to mention the outdoor work like weeding the garden, clipping the hedge and mowing the lawn. She'd push herself, worship like. Every day. I just wanted to help. Do my fair share or do it together, but she liked to glory in telling me how much pain she was in as a result of her hard work.

She said she hated the house. Never had a good word to say about it during the whole fifty years she'd lived in it. It hated her too. I know this because it told me. That proud Victorian residence built from old granite and oak, surrounded by an acre of lawn and substantial shrubbery, deserved more love. She didn't appreciate it or show it enough feeling. It was just another nuisance to her, like me – the whinging child. Even though I was in my thirties.

Everyone in the village admired the house. It was the envy of many, standing tall on a conical mound overlooking the estuary and salt marshes. Even the few tourists that visited the area would comment on the beautiful house on the hill. The grey granite gazed forth from a garlanded haze of wisteria in summer, whilst in winter it stood warrior strong, braving the wind and salt spray of the angry sea, that swirled and charged inland to crash into river water pouring from the hills. I felt safe inside. Protected and sheltered. The house was everything to me. My heart and my home.

Legend tells of an old oak tree that once grew where the house now stands, the Pagan Tree. It was worshipped by the villagers long before the old ways were battered out of them. Rags and charms had been hung in the oak's branches as wishes for the Green Man of the oak to grant. Lovers would meet under his boughs to fornicate, making fresh faced babes. Childless widows or spinsters were granted a swollen belly and hearty child in return for a token, and nobody questioned the

Green Man's right.

When the mighty oak was felled by a wealthy reverend in 1823, the villagers protested. The reverend took no notice. He wanted a larger, grander rectory for his new pompous little wife. Regardless of the curses and warnings bestowed upon him he proceeded to chop the old oak down, claiming to end such heathen ways.

"God is the power and the glory. In his name I will fell this foul fiend of the Devil, used to trick and lure the foolish into sin," he was famously quoted to have said.

The wood then became part of the house – the basic structure that created the skeletal foundations and huge beams that line the ceilings. The finer bits were used for the floorboards, wood panelling and the staircase. I imagine they would have been like sweet honey, a fresh golden colour, but age has matured them into a deeper, darker beauty. How a single tree could have produced so much useable timber I don't know, but it remains the heart and soul of the house, with acorns and oak leaves carved into the newel posts and banisters, that dominate the entrance hall.

The reverend wasn't very successful or liked in the village, and according to the records his wife died in childbirth along with his only child. He didn't stay long after that and soon left for the city. Some say he went mad and ended his days in Bedlam. The house lay empty for years before being purchased by an elderly widow; she lived alone until her death, which was well into her nineties. Then my father bought it, when mother was pregnant with me.

The house obviously appreciated the constant care and upkeep Mother poured into it, but it craved more. Not even Dad's tragic death could make her understand. He had died in the house; fell down the ladder from the loft. The house did it for her sake. It was desperate to please her, eager for the smallest piece of attention she could spare.

Mother had moaned and shouted at Dad so much over the years. The house thought it was doing her a favour, when it shook the ladder and nudged his foot to miss the vital rung. There was no acknowledgment of thanks on her part. Oh no, just another outpouring of hate aimed at the high ceilings and solid beam that had cracked Dad's head.

I know my troublesome existence, as she called it, infuriated her. Sometimes I just wanted some motherly company and conversation. She would be polite, but the initial "Oh what do you want now? I've just sat down for some peace. I haven't stopped all day!" exclamation backed up with a pained expression and forced smile, never failed to make me feel guilty. She would get up grasping her hip and gasp with pain, ignoring my futile cries of, "Please don't get up, I'll put the kettle on, or I can go if you'd prefer?" So, the house and I wallowed in guilt and found comfort in each other's failings.

I was thirteen and struggling with puberty when I realised the house wanted more. My thoughts fluttered as I thought about a boy I fancied at school. Dizzying tremors awoke in my groin flipping my stomach, and I squeezed my legs together. Taking off my clothes I pressed my nakedness against the cold granite walls and felt my nipples harden.

Excitement flickered between my thighs igniting a deep surge that shocked me. I rubbed myself against the door frame, sliding my legs either side. Feeling silly and suddenly self-conscious I tried to stop but the house wouldn't let me. My body struggled as the hard wood rubbed back and forth, and I began to panic. I soon learned to give the house what it wanted.

Sometimes I thought Mother knew what the house and I shared, and it disgusted her. She'd often look at me with an objectionable lemon lips expression. I always dreaded asking her to babysit my son Peter. Occasionally she'd agree, but not without causing me to feel shameful and dirty.

I had planned to go on a date this weekend, because I'd met someone. He'd asked me at the local library where I work. I'd seen him a few times, attempting to make eye contact through his floppy fringe. His name was Johan. His surname was Scandinavian or something, and he lived locally, according to his library account. Usually I ignored him, because his hair was a little long and he seemed a bit scruffy.

Having just shelved a load of new romances – much to the

delight of two elderly ladies – I was about to have a break. That's when he touched my arm as I passed, stopping me in my tracks.

"Umm hi," he said. "Lovely place to work, surrounded by books all day."

"Yes, if you like reading that is," I replied a little nonchalantly.

"Have you worked here long?"

"Too long. I'm just going for a break did you want something?" I snapped.

"Yes…urrmm would you…?"

I was losing patience and had started to shuffle my feet. I was bursting to pee too which didn't help.

"Look if you would excuse me, I really need to…" I began, hoping to get away.

"Would you go for a drink…with me?" he stammered.

"What?" I asked, thinking I must have misheard.

"A drink…this Saturday?" he said.

"A drink? Like a date or something?" I questioned.

"Yes. That's if you're umm not with anybody. Are you?"

"No, no. I mean yes…umm…no." I was stammering now.

"You're with someone, sorry. God…just ignore me. I just…"

"No, I mean yes to the date. No, I'm not with anyone." I managed to reply.

"Oh right, so you'll come?" he said smiling.

"I'll have to let you know; can I call you later this week?"

"Yes of course." He got his phone out to exchange contacts, but I didn't want to give him mine. Not yet.

"I have your number; it's on the library computer under your account," I said instead.

"Oh yes, of course. Do you need my name to look me up?"

"I think you're the only Johan in town. I'll call you later this week. Now I really must go." And I ran to the toilet before wetting myself. I watched him afterwards, strolling through the car park and out onto the main road. His hair blew in the wind. Mother would hate him.

I was looking forward to going out and getting to know him,

so I broached the subject to Mother about babysitting Peter. I love being with the house, but I get lonely too. Most of my friends from school are married and whenever they do invite me to anything, I feel they're only doing so out of pity. Mother was working in the greenhouse where the tomatoes were beginning to ripen. I breathed their sweetness, heightened by the late afternoon sun, as I tried to formulate my words.

"I met a nice young man at work the other day." I attempted to make my voice sound natural, hoping she wouldn't notice the quiver. She stared at me, the infamous lemon lips beginning to form. Hastily I continued. "Well, he's asked me out on a date this Saturday, so I was wondering if you…if you could look after Peter for me?"

"Why? Surely you're not going to sleep with him straight away, are you?" She looked me up and down with distaste, the lemon lips in full force.

"What? Mother…shut up please…of course I'm not." I glanced around feeling shame blush across my cheeks.

"Well, it wasn't that long ago when you were out with that other man, and look what happened there, an illegitimate child that's what."

"Peter isn't illegitimate…we were going to get married…"

"Oh really? I'll believe it when I see it."

Feeling sick, I watched as some of the overripe tomatoes squashed between her fingers. She cast these distastefully aside just like she threw my failed relationship into the dirt. I pursed my own lips in an effort not to cry. How was I to know he was only after one thing? I'd fallen in love. I believed him when he said he'd marry me, even though we'd only been together three weeks before I got pregnant. He broke my heart. I'd cried for months.

The house had been the only one to show me any sympathy after he left. It told me what I should do. So, I called the rat up one night, to ask if he'd replace one of the roof slates which had blown down. He'd not wanted to but felt obliged. To ease the guilt of leaving me pregnant and unmarried no doubt. He'd come over saying he didn't want trouble but would sort the slate and go. I laughed, as the house shrugged him off the ladder like a rag doll. He might have survived, if the granite window surround hadn't made sure it caught his temple, splitting his skull on the way down. I watched the house absorb the blood, as it seeped over the stone.

Struggling to compose myself after Mother's rebuke, and the uncomfortable memory of Peter's father, I said, "Look if I'm out for the evening I need you to babysit Peter. Can you do that for me?"

"No," she said. "I'm going to the opening of that new gallery. Sorry." Her lemon lips twisted a smile sucking tomato pulp from her fingers.

I seethed. Returning to the house I pressed my face into the solid oak mantle, above the cold grate and cried. The wood was damp and salty. I licked it, feeling the house convulse as my heart trembled. I called Johan to cancel our date. He didn't answer, so I left a message giving a lame excuse about feeling unwell. He didn't know about Peter yet, but I doubt he'd still be interested. The house told me I'm too good for him anyway.

Mother, true to her word, has left for the gallery opening, saying she isn't sure what time she'll be home. Peter is in his room playing and I'm alone with the house. We've spoken and, like me, it's had enough. I trail my fingers over the walls and rub my body against the door posts, lifting my dress to pleasure myself. Spent, I slip down pooling my body onto the floor and listen to it whisper about Mother's treatment of me…and how it's waiting for her to come home. Anger swirls along the oak beams and I can feel it pulsing through the hard stone walls and vibrating through the panelling. The house can be menacing when provoked… poor Mother.

Mother still isn't home, and it's gone ten, which has agitated the house even more. I can feel the floorboards tremble with silent pacing as it waits. We both know we'd be better off without her. *Mother will have to go* whisper the walls, *a sacrifice for the greater good.* Mother always told me I had to make sacrifices for the greater good. I had a bottle of wine with dinner and can't help hitting the Scotch now. I know I'm drinking too much, but it's hardly my fault. I dribble some onto the dark oak floor and watch the house lick it dry.

As a child I'd often share my food with the house. Hiding morsels and treats so it would have a chance to appreciate them before Mother cleaned the gifts away. It was part of what bound us together, this giving and receiving. Our tastes grew over the years, as we explored each other's cravings and desires, our relationship developing. I felt like nobody else loved me. Not with the same intensity as the house, which would do anything to ease my pain, protect me, and give me pleasure.

It's gone quiet upstairs, so I creep up to peep in on Peter and say goodnight. He's asleep. Tucked himself in like a good boy. I hated it when Mother failed to say goodnight to me, which was pretty much every night if I'm honest. In the end I'd give up waiting and fall asleep to the creaks and groans of the house taking the form of a lullaby. It was always eager to comfort me, unlike Mother. The groans would rumble and guide me to a land of green forests. I'd nestle into the woodland floor breathing the earthy scents, as woody fingers played with my hair and stroked my skin until it tingled.

I stroke Peter's hair as he sleeps, and I wonder if he too senses the house's presence. I don't think he does, he's not like me when I was little. I lean in to kiss his forehead but knock his lamp over. Cursing I pick it up and leave. I'm pissed now, so I'd best not wake him. He doesn't like it when I'm drunk. He blames me for everything…the little sod.

I see it in his eyes when he looks at me, like he knows better. Mother's eyes, I call it. Like he's judging me. The house will put him straight I'm sure… but not tonight. Tonight, its Mother's turn. I can hear the front door open, and my lips curve a smile. A pulse beats through the walls, the floors tremble with rage and Mother's footsteps falter in the hallway.

Author note: 'Heart and Home' reminds me of a beautiful house I saw near the Teifi estuary. I imagined the house taking on a persona of its own from the old oak tree that once stood in its place. This also deals with the sometimes strained and difficult relationships between mothers and daughters and touches upon mental illness that can result from, or be worsened, by rejection and childhood neglect.

# Weep Willow Weep

I hadn't understood the meaning of love before. Not the kind of helpless love you feel when you know something is wrong and you shouldn't be feeling that way, but you just can't help it. It's an unconditional love that all but consumes you. Even though deep down you know you should despise the source because it horrifies and exhausts, yet you will never willingly send the culprit away. The very fact it loves you back, no matter how desperate or needful, prevents you, and is the reason you take care of them, regardless of what others may think.

I once loved simply the sunlight and the dreamy hum of bees, the cool moist earth and the singing stream, her voice always clear and shrill in spring, lazy and seductive in summer and powerful as rock in winter. I have rested many years upon this mossy bank listening to her song whilst breathing an unblemished contentment. The warm sun changing to cool rain would wake pleasurable shudders as I felt water running rivulets down my body to leave me cleansed and replenished, and I loved it. But nothing had prepared me for the strange love I was yet to discover, a dark and frightening emotion I could not willingly escape.

A young girl, fraught with suffering began to visit me daily. She would nestle close, her tears sinking through my calloused skin, and I would drink down her pain, absorbing her disquiet. It left me lost and confused, lonely and wanting. Heartbreak is the name she gave it, and rightly so because I could feel her heart flicker and falter in its rhythm. I wanted to give her mine so hers could rest a while, to ease the anguish that pulsated from her frail and delicate life. I wanted to restore her peace and remove her sadness replacing it with joy.

Her name was Willow. I knew this because I heard raised voices, angry calls searching, but they never found her hideout. I kept her hidden, gave her the time she needed to weep and hiccup, choking back cries until spent she would sleep, the tension slowly seeping from her body. Humming deeply, I'd join my voice to the stream that whispered alongside and together we would sooth her skipping heart so the soft beating could resume a steady pace. When rested she would wake and leave me cold and alone, with a little piece of heartache lingering as I longed for her presence once more.

One day she came to me with clouded eyes. Her pace staggered and she all but fell into my embrace. I felt it instantly – venom swirled in her blood, seeking her heart, ready to end its pain, and I realised she had ingested poison to end the suffering. I tried my best to share my breath, but her life had begun to seep away before she'd even reached my side. There was nothing I could do except hold her close and sing her name as the potent toxin did its work and she succumbed.

Her soul slipped quietly from the once living flesh and I reached for her. Lulled by my voice she returned my touch, and we became one for just a moment. Her light shone brightly, and she saw me for what I was. I hid my face but felt her love move through me and the pain that had driven her to the poison lifted, releasing her into the air. I watched the silver soul motes rise and disperse as my leaves brushed the cold dead girl tangled in my roots. They still call her name, searching, but Willow has flown. Her body rests with me now, weeping into the water.

As anger left the searcher's calls they turned to pleas laced with false concern. I shrouded the cold form, whilst their cries faded into the approaching night, becoming more distant until they stopped altogether. I held my love, absorbing her death, feeling the empty silence, remembering her sweet heart, and how I would heal the ache deep within. Confused, I detected a faint beat remained. How could this be? I had seen her soul leave the useless carcass nestled in my roots. I had felt her life lift to fly forth leaving the body behind, but there was something else... A spark remained. A tiny beat, barely there, slowly grew as I poured my life energy into it, willing it to strength.

I could feel a rumbling of unease in my roots. There were other ancients in the forest, old gods like me, nature spirits, deities long forgotten by the modern world. I could sense their displeasure at what I was doing, they warned me to let the spark be, it would soon go out and I could drink the nourishment soaking into the earth. Even my beloved stream trickled her warnings, swirling and splashing my leaves, It is not her, she cried, just a dying offspring. But I didn't heed the old spirits' advice and continued to share my life, pouring it freely, fanning the little spark, eager to ignite and strengthen the tiny beating pulse.

Deep inside the rotting flesh, another life lay hidden and nourished by my pagan efforts, it slowly began to grow. I sang to the other as I had Willow, but in return a need both deep and primal reached for me. Hunger. It screamed, demanding to feed, but sunlight, earth and water was not enough for the small pale creature that was emerging. I watched aghast as it tore through flesh and sinew, screams like piercing shrieks erupting from lungs made strong by the hammering rhythm of its heart, that I had willed to life.

Tiny fists pummelled my bark, and a wet circle of a mouth sucked at the beetles sharing my skin, squeezing them between soft pink gums. I sang and rumbled, rocking slowly to sooth and quiet the raging form, but its need was too great. When its cries distressed me enough, I told it to take from the decomposing flesh it had lain within. As I had taken nourishment from the dead leaves and decaying limbs of my ancestors to grow and live, it too did the same and soon consumed my poor Willow. Her once beautiful body was now nothing but sustenance and food for another.

I sheltered the naked beast, its skin slippery with slime and warmed it with my roots. Sleep soon followed, its need now sated, and I wondered at the strange protective sensation, so akin to love, I was experiencing. On waking it grovelled and fed once more. With the flesh almost gone it begun to gnaw and suck on the bones, relishing the juices of fresh decay. On finishing, its shrieks continued and I tried to soothe the curious thing, but it ignored my futile attempts, its craving to feed both urgent and terrible, leaving me at a loss at what to do.

I began to fear it; how could I care for such a creature? I tried to calm it using the only gift I had, to lull and console easing sorrow and despair, creating tranquillity amid my peaceful roots and boughs, but to no avail. The yearning that emanated from the tiny beast was primitive, the demands clamorous. I dipped my leaves to tickle and delight, but it grabbed and snatched tearing and ripping, then hollering when realising my leaves were not filled with blood. I could do no more, my poor Willow was gone and in her stead a monster had arisen of my own making. Yet, a feeling I found hard to distinguish, flowed from me stirring my emotions.

I watched as it crawled from my tangled roots to catch and kill a mouse scuttling across the forest floor. It's mouth still held no teeth, but the gums were strong, and it crushed the bones with ease to reach the soft innards that dribbled over its chin. The kills grew larger as the beast grew stronger, crawling about with uncanny speed to pounce on and devour an unsuspecting victim, be it rabbit, squirrel or even a blackbird braving the forest floor. None escaped, the fear rising too late to flee.

Watching it suck, slurping on blood and flesh, I began to recognise the strange feeling and emotion as love. Unconditional love was what I felt for this bewildering creature that had grown inside my Willow.

I delighted when it sought me mewling and tearful if its kill struck back causing pain, my soothing humming and warm roots all it needed to console its distress. It slept too, cradled in my woody embrace and during sleep it giggled when I tickled with my leaves. I marvelled at the tiny heart beating forth such strength compared with the tiny flutter I had nurtured and breathed to life. Wriggling and gurgling, it snuffled adorably but soon dreams of hunger crept into its mind before once again waking and screaming for blood.

This changeable behaviour unnerved me, and I began to retreat when it woke, pulling my mind away, weary of the violent need to feed. I had existed for many years and lulled many souls to sleep in tranquillity beneath my leaves, but never had I felt such a burning demand for life, with such a desperate need to feed and survive, from something so small.

One warm summer's day I heard a woman's voice trilling in song. She sat by the stream to dip her toes. I had not seen another being for some time having shrouded my existence in mist to hide the creature, but as the sun rose high, I let my guard slip to revitalise my being. My leaves stretched reaching and unfurling to absorb the sunlight as my roots dug deep drinking in moisture. I felt like a willowy sapling once more, not the hunkering behemoth I had become. My mind reached to mingle with the woman's emotions as my voice joined the stream's song. Foolishly, I lulled the woman to my side where, enchanted, she rested upon the green mossy bed that covered the old dead bones of my Willow that lay amongst my roots.

I had forgotten the beast in that moment, so strong was my desire to hold the woman in my crooked limbs and sing to her gentle soul. It had begun to wander further afield to hunt, its hunger never sated for long and I gave it not a thought. How I had missed this simple seduction and the delicate minds of women, instead of the primal demands of the beast. Sleepily she succumbed to my luring caress, our voices blending with the trickling stream as she breathed the fresh scent of honeysuckle and dozed beneath my shaded canopy.

I felt her chest rise and fall as entangled within my own seductive spell I continued to sing, soothing any distress that dared rise through the mists of her mind. Her emotions were soft and simple, her troubles mere trifles compared with my Willow, and I began to remember how my life was before. How simple it had been to feel only the pleasures of the heart, to soothe any woes, to breathe in contentment and joy releasing any hurt, to watch it dissipate and become no more.

I should have been aware of my folly; I should have known... but I realised too late. The beast had returned and as the woman slept it made its kill. Stealthily creeping through the soft green moss its blood-streaked body slithered over my roots. I cried out in warning, my voice a crack of branches amidst shaking boughs and the helpless swishing of leaves, but the monster tore her throat to greedily drink the hot crimson spring. I absorbed the blood too, as it dripped through the loamy earth to soak into my roots.

Bloated we held the dying woman, my monster and me, to the slow lament of death and I wept for her life that flowed between us, revitalizing and energising. I had created a demon, whose heart beat with the timeless infusion of an old god, but whose nature and hunger sprang from the instinctual demands of man. Yet, even as the other ancients frowned upon me, my love held fast for the being I'd raised and breathed to life from the body of a poor weeping girl.

As the beast grew, learning to totter on legs made strong from blood, I applauded its life force. In time it could run and leap, pouncing on prey, showing no mercy. I knew it would leave one day to journey to the world of man, and I feared the harvest it would reap – yet part of me rejoiced. The world of man had long forgotten the power lingering in the old forests they desecrate so freely. The other ancients still berated my foolishness, calling it an abomination, but the earth drank deeply from the blood it spilt, mirroring the sacrifices of old.

I knew when the sun dipped leaving a russet tinge in the sky, and my leaves began to brown, crisping in the autumn wind preparing for the winter death, that the beast would set forth. The time had come and as the hunter's moon raised her head, I watched my creation slink into the night: The body of a man infused with the essence of a pagan god. I shivered at what was to come, and as the earth turned away from the long summer months to welcome the approach of midwinter, the veil thinned and other beings, darker creatures, slipped through from the hidden realms sensing the chaos unleashing.

The old ones stirred as those that had long succumbed to sleep felt the energy ignite, waking them from slumber. On the periphery shadows swarmed and followed the demon I had nurtured. I bristled and shook raising my head to watch it pass through the trees, a feeling of pride flowing through my roots, and I felt the old ones acknowledge what I had done. None of them had dared to challenge mankind's hold over the earth or the power of the false god, yet I had awoken a spark that would do just that.

Like a dark stream the creatures flowed through the forest, following my beast towards the twinkling lights that led to the world of man. Although I feared it, I also worshipped its monstrous existence. It was my creation and mine to love, regardless of what it would yet unleash on the world. An unconditional love was what I felt for my abomination, whether I wished it or not. Yet I still weep for the soul of my Willow, and the girl who died that warm summer's day. Their bones lie together now, nestled safely in the hollow of my roots, weeping into the water.


Author note: This story is written from the point of view of an old willow tree. Inspired by Tolkien's Old Man Willow, I wrote about unconditional love. The young girl, possibly raped and abused by her family that pursue her, leaves behind a piece of herself – an unborn child. Nourished by the old tree's ancient spirit the baby grows into a beast, half man and half god. Yet the kind old tree, although repulsed by the actions of this strange creature, nurtures it and loves it unconditionally as it would a child.

# The Islanders

The naked cry of a curlew streaks across a beach, tinged pink in the evening sun, amid the jeer of gulls and oyster catcher shrieks. It slides shyly through the tavern window to disperse tentatively across your shoulders and down your spine. Your bag packed and ready to leave waits accusingly by the door. How did it come to this? You were supposed to be healing. This place was meant to be your ticket to feeling well again, putting the past behind you. When you heard you'd inherited the little cottage from your real father, the one you'd never met, it seemed a blessing in disguise, a paradise where you could come for holidays when things got too much. Who wouldn't love a fisherman's cottage on a remote island?

The islanders had been friendly to begin with, Anna especially; you'd secretly dreamt about the possibility of romance. You held on to the thought like a pearl caught deep in your oyster heart, something precious and hidden but once revealed even better to share – but not now. Now they all looked at you with pity in their eyes, shaking their heads. Your pearl never was a pearl, just an irritating grain of sand. The old lady behind the bar had patted your shoulder muttering something about too much sun and local whisky doing funny things to people. Best get home, get well again. The doctor said you had a concussion from when you hit your head, he'd stitched the wound, but you are to go to your GP as soon as you get back. He would contact them to let them know what happened, and tell them how unhinged you are, no doubt.

It had been a pleasant surprise to find the cottage was so well kept when you arrived, you'd thought it would be derelict, but one of the islanders had been looking after it. It wasn't your original plan, but after today you've arranged a quick sale to him. He's here tonight, in the bar downstairs, celebrating the day's haul. They're all here, like they are every weekend. The women who never wear a scrap of make-up all week, turn up like painted whores reeking of cheap perfume to disguise the stink of fish – although tonight it disguises the stench of burning, and the men act like debauched fools. It amused you at first but after today you're sickened.

It happened in the morning, when you took a walk on the beach. Some of the fishing boats came back dragging their nets behind them...

Stopping to watch and hoping to witness some traditional island life, you sit, feeling rough barnacles press into the muscles of your back as you stretch your legs and lean comfortably against the rocks. The bright sun burns hot on your face whilst the warm white sand reflects a pale moonlight. The boats bob as the turquoise sea swells and wanes beneath them. The men struggle with the nets making white ripples that slice through the blue as they drag them to shore

It's an ethereal vista untouched by tourism where nature resides in abundance. Black-backed and herring gulls caw and scuff in the clear sky, hovering over the boats eager for fish, and for the first time in months you think of your mother and wonder why she never spoke about this place or brought you here as a child; she adored birds and this was a bird lover's paradise. You think of your real father and wonder, not for the first time, why he never sought you out. A Great Skua swoops into the flock of gulls and bullies them aside, and they screech and tussle whilst further along the shore gannets dive like silver pendants plummeting into a jewelled sea.

As the fishing boats draw closer you notice the nets look heavy. At first you think they've caught a few small sharks or seals perhaps. Feeling intrigued and a little concerned, you keep watching. A slow feeling of dread begins to trickle into your senses, and then becomes a torrent as fascination turns to shock. Removing your sunglasses you wipe them on your shirt and rub your eyes. Why is nobody reacting? They're just getting on with it as normal, haven't they noticed?

The torrent inside your head roars like a waterfall as you shout out demanding they stop what they're doing. You run down to the shore and wade into the crystal waters to stare in horror whilst the islanders grin dumbly at you. Your distress at their behaviour seems to amuse them. The chap you sold the cottage to said he was a kid the last time they had a haul like this; his father had helped drag the nets in – mine too apparently. Laughing, his arms tensing like ropes popping out of wet sand, he pulls the nets in.

They were half fish, the things in the nets. What you mean is, they were human – and animal – and half bloody fish. They dragged them onto the beach, long withered ugly faces, some clearly human and others like beasts. They were dying and some were already dead. Running closer in disbelief you think your brain will react in a minute and you'd see that they are large fish or seals – but they're not. This isn't like any psychosis you have known before. Even in your darkest days of delirium you have never experienced anything like this.

The islanders bring large piles of driftwood and kindling and stack it up on the beach. They drag the creatures towards it and lay them on top. You stare hopelessly as a young woman – well, she had the torso of a young woman – is thrown onto the top of the pile. Her tail or fin whatever it is catches on a piece of pointed wood, her torso slips down, and she hangs there helpless. Her flesh is unblemished like alabaster, her breasts small mounds with no nipples, just patches of pink mother of pearl. The pale torso morphs into the scaly tail of a fish but green liquid not blood oozes out of the wound where the wooden hook has trapped her.

Falling to your knees you retch as your eyes seek out her face and hope she is, after all, just a shark or dead seal – something you can recognise that comes from the sea. Her long hollow face is draped in dark green seaweed which you realise is hair. Kneeling like a priest before his altar you look up and into her eyes. There is no white or pupil, just a deep glistening opal, a universe both huge and tiny all at once. A vast empty ocean to fall into before disappearing… and you understand: she is from the sea, but something you've only read about in fairytales and legend.

The islanders laugh at you as they drag more of the creatures forward. One had the front of a white horse. Pitifully it struggles to get away, but someone sticks a knife in its throat and greenish liquid bubbles out leaving a long emerald stain, green against pearl white. Its eerie eyes flicker and turn grey. They heft it onto the pile, and you see the half fish woman still hanging, her face etched with sorrow, as she reaches down to tenderly stroke what would have been the forelock had it been a normal horse. Surely these creatures need help – they could be a new species unknown to mankind, you yell, and beg the islanders to stop.

Nobody listens and the last thing you remember before, you're certain, someone bashed you over the head, was staring at the strange iridescent tails of these wondrous beasts as the islanders set fire to the pile of wood. Their mouths open wide as if screaming but you hear no sound. Some of the dogs that had been hanging around hoping for food run off whimpering. Struggling, you try to stand and reach into the flames to grab the long pale hand, desperate to help, to save, to rescue, to stop the slaughter, to end the suffering. The islanders hoot and cheer. Pain attacks your skull like water exploding through the walls of a cave and oblivion swoops down to gather you into her wicked wings.

The memory is all too real; grabbing your bag you leave the tavern, avoiding the bar and the drunken islanders. Heading for the last ferry back to the mainland you ignore the whimpering cries of the curlew echoing pleadingly behind.

'The Islanders' was published by Parthian books in an anthology entitled *Heartland,* the result of a competition and a 'celebration of writing and writers.' I experimented with writing in second person, where the protagonist's unstable mind and crippling anxiety leads to horrific visions on a remote island. It is a painful tale and unfortunately all too true when humanity sees itself as superior over the natural world even when they don't yet understand the implications of their actions.

# Hunted

I remember running in the snow with my brother, playing and rolling about careless to the cold. It was mid-winter's eve, and we had everything to live for. Then they came. My brother and I ran home. We told Mother, and she told us to stay out of sight, that she'd lead them away from our home and double back. She'd done it before, she told us confidently. We had nothing to fear, as long as we didn't get seen, and then she was gone. I never saw my mother again.

They came for us just before dark. We tried to make a run for it, but they netted us. We were plunged into a soggy blackness, a sack or something strong that wouldn't tear even though we struggled to get out. I could hear an engine starting and knew we were being taken somewhere. My brother was crying. I'd never seen him cry and I could smell the sharp stench of ammonia and knew we had both soiled ourselves. I could smell others too and hear them, whimpering. We were not the only ones.

They threw us onto a cold floor still in the sack; it was hard and smelt of death. Rough hands wrenched open the top. Sharp eyes peered and a flash of white teeth grinned. I turned my face into the coarse material not wanting to see. Moments later a heavy door closed, and I heard footsteps receding.

Cautiously my brother wriggled out of the sack and frantic to stay close I followed. We were in a box of some sort with barely enough room for the two of us. Claw marks gouged deep in the wood foretold of previous occupants that had suffered our fate. There were similar boxes next to us and I could hear others moving and crying. My brother and I hadn't spoken, only shared anxious glances. I suppose it was shock. In the corner was a heavy ceramic bowl of water. It was filthy and tasted sour but we both drank a little.

Not knowing what would happen we curled up together. I hid my face in my brother's shoulder. I could smell fear on him. He curled around me, and we lay there, our breaths shallow as we awaited the fate our captors had planned. We were not stupid, we knew it was just sport for them, and our suffering only made it better. We'd heard the stories, tales told at the time of the winter solstice. We had listened trembling, snuggling up together nice and cosy hoping it would never happen to us. Mother would shush the others, telling us not to listen to such evil things. Just old fairytales, she'd say.

Our internal body clock was used to being awake at dawn, so we were ready when they came. We huddled in the back of the box. A man cursed as he reached in to grab one of us. My brother pushed me behind him and stood his ground. His breath snarled through his lips, but they put something around his neck and dragged him out. He kicked and I tried to grab him, but something hit me in the face. I heard him cry out as the door slammed shut. I screamed for him – we'd never been separated before.

There were lots of vehicles arriving, their engines rough and hoarse. Then I heard the dogs, slavering howls and frantic barking. My brother, my poor beautiful brother, was out there with them. I scrabbled in the box. I scratched and fought against the splinters, adding my own gashes in the wood alongside my predecessor's futile attempts. A horn sounded and I knew what they were going to do. Run little brother, I prayed, run. Rocking back and forth I cried, my heart open and raw as I realised what had happened to my mother was now happening to my brother.

I was numb with shock and fear. Lacking the energy to move to the corner to relieve myself I lay covered in my own excrement and begged the mid-winter spirit to grant my brother a quick death. Through my own whines the echo of vehicles approached once more. I heard others cry out in fear. Blue lights flashed through the tiny cracks in the box. Whatever horror was waiting I would not run, and I wouldn't fight. I wouldn't give them the pleasure. There were voices, urgent exclamations and the pounding of feet. Something was different. I could feel a change in the air. I lifted my head, straining to listen.

A soft tread approached and weak with fright I lay frozen. Slowly the door to my box opened, just a crack, and a light flashed, blinding me. I flinched, closing my eyes but a soft voice spoke.

"It's okay, we've found you now, don't be afraid." I felt a wash of soothing vibrations flood over me and knew they came from the man who had opened my box. Confused at this show of empathy and kindness I half opened my eyes, doubting my senses, fearing a trap.

"We've another youngster here; it'll have to go straight to the vet by the look of it. Has the van from the wildlife hospital arrived?"

"Yes. Hell of a thing, who'd imagine with the ban on hunting these sickos would catch young uns and lock them up to hunt at their leisure?"

"You'd be surprised what some people think they can get away with." Both voices held a different tone to my captors, and I felt a wave of empathy stir and muddle my senses. The urge to flee was still insistent but I allowed myself to be removed from my prison and placed in soft blankets and gently passed to another. I could sense the hands that took me were feminine, I could smell the scent change but still the vibrations were kind.

"Another youngster with not much strength left. Poor little thing." The voice was gentle, and I shuddered, my body confused. "She's a female, and apart from shock and exhaustion I don't think she's damaged. Make sure you arrest whoever's responsible."

"I most certainly will," replied the man.

I felt myself transferred to a warm place and waited as other survivors were brought to safety. My eyes fluttered with exhaustion, my heart's erratic beating slowed, my breaths came shallow and shuddering as they calmed and my body succumbed to sleep. I thought of my brother and as the fog of fear cleared, I knew that somewhere he was watching.

'Hunted' was published by The League Against Cruel Sports, in *Protect* magazine. As an avid anti-hunt supporter, I wrote this to hold accountable the evil that has been and is still being committed against our wonderful wildlife, and the cruelty mankind is capable off. The kidnap of baby foxes is something British foxhunts have been exposed to doing under the cover of so-called blood-free drag hunts. I praise the good work being done all over the country by the League and other anti-hunt support groups: you are the voice and the hope of the hunted and abused.

# My Spirit and I

The Dead Woods were called this because nothing grew at the foot of the monstrous beech trees that towered above. Their canopies created a dappled glow, mottling the copper carpets. Apart from the name, it was the most magical place, and it was there I first saw him, stumbling among the bony trunks, lame and scarred. His fur was a dirty piss-coloured yellow, with encrusted faeces hanging in clumps from his hind legs and belly, like he'd been sleeping in his own shit. In fact, he looked much like I felt. Crap.

I'd grown up with horses having been a trainer in my younger days, but since my own horse died of old age a few years ago, I felt I couldn't do it anymore. I was old and stiff now, but I missed my boy. He'd been thirty-one when he'd passed over the Rainbow Bridge, as my daughter called it. Now with my daughter away, having married a foreigner, and her father a distant mistake, I found myself alone and miserable.

I approached the desecrated beast, my shoulders slumped, avoiding eye contact to appear non-confrontational, and spoke soothing *whoas, steady there,* phrases that slipped easily from my throat. He startled slightly but was so emaciated he had no energy for flight or fight. Ribs poked proud of a protruding spine, and an array of savage scars criss-crossed his hat-racked pelvis, like the carvings in the beech trunks.

Pale blue eyes crusted and sore, with the fleshy pink membranes blistered red, told me he was a *cremello* coloured horse. I realised the scars looked so fresh because his skin was pale pink, like all cremellos. His coat only looked a dirty yellow because of the dullness, when it should be shimmering like ivory silk. You poor, poor thing, I murmured, edging closer to brush my hand against his shoulder.

I had an empty paddock sitting at the side of my house, with a grey stone marking the place my horse had been buried. I'm sure he wouldn't mind sharing the paddock until the authorities had been notified. Hopefully the owners/breeders could be traced, and whoever was responsible for such neglect brought to account.

Slowly, I removed my belt and slid it around his neck so I could lead him the short walk home. He plodded alongside, head lowered and defeated. Cracked and overgrown hooves tripped his stiff legs, as he walked woodenly. I smoothed his face, and he flinched, eyes rolling with deep-seated fear. It's okay, I soothed, not wanting to startle him until he was in the paddock, where a vet could check him over.

Safely contained, he dropped his head to smell the grass. Cornflower eyes watched me through a mane heavy with fairy knots. I ran my hand through my own hair, realising it wasn't much better. I gave him a bucket of fresh water and slowly he drank. The cool liquid dribbled from his lips when he lifted his head to regard me, sighing, accepting my presence.

I drove into town and called at the veterinary surgery. The vet was busy, out on a call, so I bought soothing eye lotion and liniment for pain and inflammation. I explained to the receptionist that I had found a loose horse and gave the description. She assured me nothing had been reported but would let the vet know and get him to call me back. I was not to worry, she assured, before helping me to my car, a strange pitying expression behind her eyes.

The vet didn't call me back, although I saw his car outside, from the bathroom window, later that next day. He was standing, hands on hips, staring into the paddock before shaking his head and returning to his car. I struggled to get dressed, hoping to speak with him before he left, but before I could make it downstairs, his car pulled away.

Spirit gazed at me from the paddock gate, looking much brighter. I'd named him Spirit, because that first night, the moon had bathed him in an ephemeral glow, his coat shimmering. I wondered if the vet had checked for a microchip and would soon find the owner. I hoped not. They didn't deserve a horse like this.

I decided to phone the vet to check, and apologise for not being around when he called over and was spoken to in that pitying tone again. They told me that little Spirit was doing well. No, he wasn't microchipped and there hadn't been any horses reported lost, and I could keep him if it made me happy. How strange, I thought, but I wasn't going to argue with getting a free horse, and such a beauty too.

Soon I began to feel my life had a purpose again. Instead of lying in bed slipping into depression, and moaning about my arthritis, I was up early caring for Spirit. I'd managed to clip most of the crusted faeces away and combed out his mane and tail. After bathing him in warm, medicated water, his skin shone rosy through his pale fur. I laughed, calling him my pink pony. I'd always wanted a pink pony as a child – or a pink unicorn. Now, that would be something.

Our relationship grew until I realised I loved Spirit, truly loved him. I had no idea if he was broken to riding or not, but one day I leaned over his back and pulled myself astride. Holding tightly to his mane my hips moved pain free, as his body heat warmed them. The sweet scent of horse relaxed me. I had no saddle or bridle, but he responded to my whispers, his ears flickering.

I rode him in the field a few times, before we braved the dead woods. I dismounted when we reached what I called the heart of the forest. Spirit rubbed his head against me, and I noticed gold flecks on my jacket. Underneath his forelock a smooth bony growth protruded shimmering golden, catching in the chequered sunlight. I touched the neat stub of a horn and marvelled at the slender beauty that gleamed with that rosy sheen. Not just a pink pony, but a unicorn too! I couldn't believe my luck.

Cries broke through my wonder, and I recognised my daughter's voice calling my name. She had phoned a couple of times, but I'd been out riding and not even bothered to return her calls. Not because I didn't want to, it was just that I'd forgotten. The vet had called too, but I didn't return any of his calls either. I just listened to his ridiculous messages, talking to me like I was a child or something. No, my daughter could wait too. I'd hide in the woods a little longer, I thought, not wanting normality to interrupt my precious time with Spirit.

I sprang easily onto Spirit's back again, my old bones less stiff. My body was becoming lithe and agile again since riding. I felt much healthier and had even stopped taking my blood pressure tablets and those other medications that left me so tired. My mind was freer, and I lived each day with vigour and purpose. Spirit was everything to me. I felt twenty years younger since he'd been in my life these past few weeks, or months – I couldn't even remember. Time seemed irrelevant.

The moon hung low and bright, and I realised night had fallen, where a few moments before it had been day. A milky beam led the way. Spirit knew where he was going because he didn't hesitate or wait for me to direct him. I clutched his mane as my body absorbed the movement, sitting easily to his stride, his back now firm and muscled. The breath of the woods embraced us, rich and damp, the forest floor soft as we turned off the track where a leafy silence wrapped its cloak around us.

Through the beech trees, moonlight glimmered in silver dapples. They twinkled like pennies against Spirit's unicorn horn, now quite pronounced. I breathed the earth scents from leaf mulch and fungi to a heady night-time floral. My senses were alive, my own spirit soaring. Ahead, an ivory path spilled a ribbon through the woods meandering between the bone-coloured beech. Spirit followed. It twisted and turned before leading to a slice in the air, where rainbow prisms peeped, and colours danced in the night.

A familiar cry echoed inside my head. Blinking I watched the light dim, the colours flee and discovered myself kneeling in the dirt, limbs stiff from the cold. Voices surrounded me, amongst them my daughter's tones, fraught with worry. Torches shone and a radio crackled; she had phoned the police on finding the house empty. They in turn, had called for an ambulance. I was taken home, checked over and told off for not taking my pills. I could hear utterances of dementia, like sparrows twittering in bushes.

My body sags now, as pain sears through seized muscles, and bones stiffen like the trunks of the beech trees, bearing the scars of life. How? I wonder. Where is my Spirit? He was right here, I tell them; didn't you see me riding like I used to, I say. Worried glances leap from my daughter, when I mention my Spirit. She blames my condition on a fall I'd had in the woods, a fall I have no recollection of having.

I am taken to hospital where those awful drugs dull my senses again. The doctors are nice enough, but it's so annoying how everyone talks to me. Like I'm a child. I worry for my Spirit and tell the nurses that I need to go home, to care for him. They tell me not to worry, that my daughter is looking after my unicorn. How did you know he was a unicorn? I ask, because I'm sure I haven't told them… unless my daughter did. This worries me. I hope nobody tries to take him away. The nurses exchange glances and continue bustling about. I can go home soon, apparently.

The day of my release from the hospital arrives and I'm feeling positive. They need the bed because there are so many other people sicker than me. I'm to have carers at home, and my daughter will be there to begin with. I'm to take my medication, they tell me. The carers will be giving it to me, and I mustn't be difficult, they say. I agree – anything to get out of this place. The drugs make me drowsy, but I'll have to comply until the time is right. My Spirit will let me know when it is.

The moon is full, and friendly smiles make me food and prepare me for bed. They lock me inside the house at night, now that the doctor has diagnosed dementia. They fear my nighttime wanderings. At first I protested and caused uproar, but dreading the care home that beckons, I have become clever and behave myself. Unbeknown to them I have an old spare key to the back door. Tonight, I will take it and find my Spirit. His voice is louder now. Colours sparkle invitingly at the corner of my vision.

I can almost smell the damp earth and fungi waiting along the moonlit path, as obligingly I finish a small bowl of tomato soup. The carers are happy, relieved I have been so easy to deal with tonight. After spitting my pills into my hand, which I've taken to doing, I say goodnight and pretend to snooze as they tuck me in. The front door closes, and a car engine starts. They believe me already asleep. I've been a good girl, complying and fooling everybody. As the thrum pulls away into the distance I leave my bed.

I only have a couple of hours before my daughter arrives to check on me. What a burden I have become. My bones are stiff, and I struggle down the stairs. The back door clicks loudly, breaking the silence, and the soft caress of night tickles my neck with a sigh. A ribbon of moonlight leads the way to a distant prism of colour. My heart thumps against my ribs and the ground trembles.

Spirit, I call, is that you? I hurry through the fields heading to the woods. My body begins to lighten as I start to run. The cold autumn night brushes over me and I don't feel the biting wind I know is blowing. Soon I won't even feel the sharp pain in my chest, or the dull ache that's thrumming through my old bones. Old bones? I'll show them, I say aloud. I just need my Spirit back. Spirit, I call, are you there?

Through the bone like trunks of the beech trees a familiar whinny greets me. Hello Spirit, I say, you look fantastic. I marvel at his gleaming horn, golden and fully formed now. Colours dance in dust motes around him and his coat ripples like silk. I find I am pain free again and easily vault onto his back, like I used to on my own horse many years ago. I sit tall and tangle my fingers into flowing strands of mane, and once more I am riding. Riding and laughing. With the wind whipping autumn leaves into my hair, my Spirit and I gallop through the dead woods and into the prisms of colour.

Author note: Alzheimer's disease and dementia frighten me. It's terrifying and bewildering and I fear it happening. 'My Spirit and I' is what I hope my own experience would be like if the inevitable happened. There is no avoiding the heartbreak left behind, but maybe if a kind Spirit appeared to guide the sufferer to their final resting, would that not be magical? I'm a horse person and miss the horses that have been present in my life and yes, when I was young, I too wanted a unicorn. Maybe my horses that have passed will appear as magical Spirits to guide me on to my next adventure – one that waits beyond the rainbow prisms. I hope so.

## My Baby He Ate Me

He embarrassed me, the way he slunk behind as I walked, claws clicking and scraping. He would never walk alongside or take my hand but then I'd flinch if he tried. I suppose it was his nature, to prowl and stalk.

The shock I'd felt when Mum came home from the hospital, she'd wept and screamed leaving me with the thing. Peeping under the cotton bonnet I recoiled as a bony face tufted with black hair, growing far too low on its forehead, grizzled. I'd quickly looked under the wrapping and relaxed a little seeing it was male.

I'd seen a female once in the next town, I was only a kid at the time, and I remember laughing and pointing. Look at the hairy legs on that, I'd yelled with my school mates as we pointed at the misshapen limbs protruding from a pink dress.

"Gerroff you fucks," her mother had said, as exhausted she'd dragged the wretch behind her.

The wretch had held back though, pulling on her mother's arm, grinning, revealing two sharp fangs nudging through bloodied gums; her nose jutted, forming a muzzle and she'd growled deep and guttural. I'd had nightmares – still do – about those teeth and the absurdity of the thing dressed in pink and frills. The virus hadn't been around long in those days.

The bundle in my arms began to wriggle so I put it on the floor, repulsed as its furry hand reached for me, nails sharp and spiky.

"Mum," I called, "it's hungry." I left it grovelling on the floorboards and went to find her.

She was slumped over the sink, expressing from heavy veined breasts. I hovered in the doorway, suddenly afraid, the rawness nauseating. Sweat ran down her face and the sickly stench of curdled milk mingled with something feral.

"Here," she said, handing me a bottle. "Feed it, I'm knackered."

"It's a boy," I said.

"Makes no fucking difference, I'm doomed either way."

I bit my lip until it bled then wiped it, suddenly conscious that the thing would smell it and want to eat me instead.

I took the bottle, retching as the milk slimed along the plastic interior, with streaks of red where Mum's blood rippled through, giving the little'un a taste of the future.

"It's his fault," screamed Mum. "That fa…"

I knew what she was going to say and quickly rose to Dad's defence. "It's not Dad's fault, he didn't know –"

"Didn't know? I bet the fucker did. How could he not 'av? And you always sticking up for him even when –"

"He wouldn't do this to us knowingly Mum," I said. "He wouldn't."

"Where the fuck is he then? He could take that little beast and find some other bitch to raise it."

She was right. Dad had fucked off. He'd had a certificate to say he was clean, like she did, but they were being forged all the time, or the virus hadn't shown on the test, that sometimes happened in the early days. I thought of myself.

"What about me, Mum?"

She looked at me with a glimmer of compassion before slamming her bedroom door.

A cry echoed from the living room ending in a series of high-pitched yelps. I took the bottle and knelt on the floor. I couldn't bring myself to pick the creature up, so I just held the teat to its face and watched. Fleshy lips revealing tiny teeth peeking from bulbous gums slurped, and sharp clawed hands scratched and scraped the plastic. Its eyes blinked a deep wolf yellow.

Not long after, we were thrown out of our house. Mum couldn't pay the rent because word had gone round about my unfortunate brother. Shunned by friends and surviving off scraps we lived on a street where others of his kind lived. I was glad of his presence then when those others licked their lips and salivated when I passed. He kind of protected me. I asked a few of them if they knew Dad but some were so far gone in the change they couldn't answer. One female told me she thought he'd gone into the woods, which is what happens when some carriers end up making the change. I hoped he had coz that way he'd not remember us and see what he'd done.

Mum refused to do anything with the beast or even name him, so rather than call him 'it' or 'thing' or anything else, I named him Mutt. In his own way I think he loved me. I thought he may eat me instead of Mum when the time came, but he knew what he was doing, and I shuddered when he got a whiff of Mum's scent and slavered. His eyes were uncannily beautiful though. They say that's the last thing the mother sees. It's what hypnotizes them and makes it pain free… Well, I hoped for Mum's sake it would be.

This is how I came to be walking through the wrong part of town with him skulking behind. I was thinking about going to see my old friends but knew Mutt would follow. They'd told me to come, that they understood but I knew when they saw him they wouldn't. But I was so tempted; just to have a drink and a chat with normal people again would be something.

Instead, I stood in the shadows on the edge of that barren place before normal life began and saw this guy around my age walking towards me. Just looking for a bit of pussy I thought and laughed then because it was only a bit of a dog he'd get round here. Some of them prostituted themselves before the change got too bad. There were men who got off on it, normal men who lingered on the edges willing to pay.

"What's that thing to you then?" he said, nodding in Mutt's direction. "You don't look sick enough to be the mother."

"I'm not. I suppose you could call him my brother," I replied.

"That's bad," he said. "So how did he come about?"

"My Dad. He must have been a carrier, said he wasn't, had that test, but… " I shrugged.

"It's changing. Outfoxing the big brains," he said. "Like the virus got cleverer."

I smiled at his choice of words. "Out-wolfing more like."

"Want a drink or something?" he asked.

I looked at Mutt who was sniffing about in the trees and began to walk away.

"No, wait," he called. "Not in a bar, but my place. I don't live far, someone's got to live on the border."

"Why so close?" I asked.

"Don't have much money, I'm not local and they treat foreigners here almost as bad as you lot," he replied.

"Hey, I'm not one of them things," I said, looking at Mutt taking a shit.

"Sorry, I meant shunned, cast out," he said, averting his eyes from Mutt's steaming pile.

What's your name?" I asked.

"Jamal," he said. "You?"

"Kim."

So, I joined him at his place. He was right when he'd said he didn't have much. I don't think he was even legally in these parts, and he did all the crap jobs other people didn't want to, but it paid the bills and afforded him a hovel to call his own. We just played cards when I visited and listened to music. He had an old record player and some scratchy records, old stuff I'd not heard before. Jamal's favourite was *Blue Moon*, the tune lodging itself like a continuous soundtrack in my head and I hummed it over and over. Ironic really.

I left Mutt outside when I called round. Couldn't bring myself to invite him in. He was getting bigger, and I was starting to fear him. He'd wait, hiding in the trees, prowling, all agitated because he wasn't with me. That was when Mum was still alive, well barely. I'll never forget the night it happened. I hadn't realised it would be so soon.

I'd been visiting Jamal and had to leave early because Mutt had been fretting, scratching at the trees and making a right ruckus. I was frightened someone would see him and then find me and I'd get Jamal into trouble, so I'd gone out and kicked the little fuck. I felt bad when he started howling, so I told Jamal I'd see him again and took Mutt home.

I could hear Mum crying, when I got in.

"What's up?" I said, scowling as Mutt pushed passed.

Mum looked rough, blood oozing out of ruptured sores, and she stank, a feral musk. I'd noticed it getting stronger and thought it was Mutt but now I realised it was Mum. I gagged, putting my sleeve over my mouth.

"I think it's going to happen Kim… don't let him… get him away." Mum fell off the sofa too weak to stand.

Mutt had gone into stealth mode slavering on all fours. His shoulder bones poked up like haunches and he growled, his face stretched muzzle like, glistening with saliva, his nose curling into a snarl.

"Oi fuck face," I yelled kicking his arse with my boot as I went to help Mum, but he snapped back, and I recoiled. His jaw looked huge, almost deformed as he swiped a claw at me.

Mum was sobbing now. Her eyes reached mine and at that moment Mutt leapt at her. She screamed as he tore her bloodied skin. He relished in the arterial blood that pumped, tilting his head back and howling before lapping. He drank and sucked, ripping chunks of flesh from her bones whilst, still alive, she kept screaming, her eyes boring into my own as I stood there helpless – the notes of *Blue Moon* whining in my head.

"Stop it… Gerroff her you bastard!" I yelled, knowing it was no good. I was too scared; Mutt had engulfed her, was consuming her. Bones snapped and shattered as his chops smacked and slavered. Her face was looking at him now, mesmerized almost, as he chewed on her innards, blue-red and visceral. That's when I ran, screaming, as he ate our mother. Others like him laughed, chanting wolf like down the street. I ran as fast as I could to Jamal's place.

He held me as I cried. I didn't have to explain what had happened because we'd talked about it, we both knew the time would come. Mutt wouldn't follow me anymore now; he'd most likely go into the woods and find Dad. That's if Dad had changed. Maybe I would change too, but not all carriers did. Jamal had assured me that I would have by now if I was going to, or at least have shown signs. Maybe I wasn't a carrier?

I lived with Jamal from then on, I never went back, and if I'm honest life improved. I kept house and he worked, and I suppose we got complacent. We couldn't help it; it was bound to happen at some point. That tender touch, a kiss here and there, our bodies flickering with desire. I knew he wanted me, so we started having sex. We were careful but somehow it happened.

My period was late, and I had no way of properly telling if I was pregnant or not. I didn't want to go to the doctor because the authorities were cracking down on potential carriers and locking them up. Some said they were being deported to god knows where. Jamal said he knew the place because it was not far from where he came from, and it was hell on earth. He beat himself up about what had happened and wept at my side. I tried reassuring him, because there was a chance we could have a normal baby.

"Shall we kill it," he'd asked. I shrugged because I wondered why I hadn't killed Mutt when he was just that grovelling mewling scrap on the floor, but I hadn't… I didn't have it in me. Then I remembered the eyes, the deep wolf yellow and I think they had power – power to stop you doing the unthinkable.

My belly grew huge, and I knew then I'd not have a normal child. It was the same with Mum, she'd been so big she went into labour early. It was always the same with the beasts.

A blue moon mocked me from the window when my labour started. Jamal was working and I'd lain for hours writhing and gasping alone. He'd arrived home just as I could feel its head pushing through. He threw his bag down and ran to me, eyes wide and fearful.

"Gerr it out of me…" I gasped, thinking of how exhausted Mum had looked when she'd come home with Mutt.

Jamal tried to calm me and held my hands. He didn't know what to say but I was glad he was there to just hold me. I screamed and strained, my nails digging into his skin, until I felt the thing slip from my body. An acrid stench rose from between my thighs, and I heard that awful growling and mewling that Mutt had made.

"Kill it…" I gasped. "Stamp on its head or something… quick, you've got to."

Jamal, crying and wiping at his eyes, placed the tiny wriggling scrawn, fur damp and bloodied, onto the floor, its snout sniffling.

"Do it... please..." I mouthed the words, nothing more than breath I was so exhausted. His gaze flickered from me to the beast and back, shock and repulsion mixed with something else – pity? – spread like a stain over his face.

"But... but Kim it's..."

"It's fuck all," I said. "Please, Jamal, do it now!"

I wanted it dead. Dead before it could suckle and taste my blood. Just as one day it would taste all of me, tearing into flesh and bone whilst I succumbed, powerless to stop the monster. It would eat me alive.

Jamal raised his boot, and I leant forward. I don't know why, some stupid instinct to see, watch its demise maybe – but involuntarily I reached for it. Jamal hesitated and those deep, wolf yellow eyes flashed between us and a pitiful whine, almost human, escaped its fleshy lips.

A smile spread like innocence across its face and tiny clawed hands stretched to play with the laces on Jamal's boot. Clicking and scratching against the leather. Click. Scratch. Click. Snuffle. Giggle.

Author note: 'My Baby He Ate Me' was written when I needed to take a break from writing and research for my PhD. I'd been looking at fairy tales, predominately The Juniper Tree also sometimes referred to as *My Mother She Slew Me My Father He Ate Me*. With this whole fairy tale theme swirling through my mind, amongst thoughts of wolves, changelings and werewolves, horror and zombie viruses, (thoughts that occupy many people's minds... I think?) this tale emerged. Another story that I would like to revisit and grow into a novel, to discover more about what's in the woods where the changeling wolves go...

# Swine

The football was on again. Chants from the roaring crowd echoed out of the TV. Every now and then Rob would jump up and yell in jubilation or shout and swear obscenities at the referee. I was not a fan. So I retreated to a corner of the terrace, a gin and tonic in hand, and watched the hot Provençal sun sink below the hills splashing the sky with orange. It was a welcome vice I had succumbed to every evening whilst watching the wild boar from the woods eat the waste food I put out for them.

I loved pigs. When I was a little girl my father bred the Tamworth, one of Britain's oldest and rarest breeds. They were lovely long-legged ginger snufflers. My hair was the same colour. We lived in a wooded area perfect for them. They had long snouts like the boar here, ideal for rummaging. They produced tasty bacon, but not long after Mummy left, I stopped eating pork. Daddy was livid, but the pigs were my friends and eating them didn't seem right anymore.

It was a real treat to have the wild boar visit my garden, which is why I encouraged them. A sow had had piglets recently and they were beginning to emerge from the undergrowth. I held my breath as first two, and then five little piggies came into the open. They snuffled and played in the potato peelings and vegetables I'd put out. A loud roar echoed through the patio doors and all the piggies scattered back to the safety of the woods. Bugger him, I thought. When I had lived alone, I craved company, but the reality of living with Rob wasn't how I envisaged it. My precious space had been well and truly invaded. His presence seemed to be everywhere and mine was shrinking.

Before Rob moved in, I would jump with anticipation at the ping of a message arriving on the laptop. We had chatted every day online, happy within our virtual little world – well I was, anyway. Then he mentioned he could work from home and planned to move to France so he could be with me. At first, I was overjoyed. A man wanted me, and not just for sex, but actually wanted to live with me. I was frightened too, frightened of losing my independence. So, I suggested he rent somewhere in the village first, but he couldn't see the point in that. A waste of money, he said, when I had this lovely little property all to myself.

I had pondered this statement but my desperation to be wanted by him and to be a normal couple overshadowed my doubts. I'd thought it just my paranoia. It couldn't possibly get as bad as my parent's relationship, but I'd never lived with anyone before. I'd had boyfriends but Daddy always made sure nothing came of it. But he was dead now. That's how I'd managed to buy this little place. I'd sold the old farm and moved out here. I'd always been good at French in school and my work as a translator allowed for my lonely existence.

My house was remote but not totally isolated. I had neighbours, an elderly Dutch couple, although they were not around often. It was their holiday home, and they had begun spending less and less time there. Rob had moved in last summer, and don't get me wrong, I had enjoyed his company. He was a lovely man and adored me, loved me even.

He had befriended the locals fitting in with ease – unlike me. I stood out like a sore thumb with my ginger mop and turned up nose. I didn't like being stared at, my looks commented on like Mummy used to. Rob's dark hair and aquiline nose blended in. He was quite attractive, but the thing was I didn't love him. I thought I did, but I know now that I didn't. His presence had begun to feel like an intruder in my quaint little woodland retreat.

The area surrounding my home was beautiful and only an hour's drive from the idyllic beaches of the Cote d'Azur. I didn't have a coastal view, unlike some of the fancier villas, but it didn't bother me. My little house was shrouded in the shadow of rocky tipped mountains draped in skirts of cork oak and pine trees. They swished right up to the garden where cheeky saplings invaded the lawn. The cork trees were what attracted the wild boar. The acorns they produced were a large part of their diet, and the food I put out for them of course. Rob said I should stop feeding them, he didn't like them. He thought they were dangerous and had once threatened to buy a gun to shoot them. I'd shoot him before he got a chance to kill any of my beloved pigs.

I jumped, spilling my drink, as a loud shout and curse from Rob interrupted my musings, and for the second time, scared the boars that had just ventured back out of the wood. Damn him, I thought getting up to refill my glass. I really didn't want him here anymore. I could try telling him I wanted him to go away, but would he listen? He was so loud and overpowering that sometimes I felt like a small mouse, my squeaks going unheard. Maybe I would do something about it tonight. I'd tell him it wasn't working. But that was my trouble, I never spoke out for myself, not against Mummy or against Daddy. But they were gone now, thank God.

I noticed, as I walked back through the lounge to get ice for my gin, the empty beer cans all over the floor, and how my little house was becoming less my little haven and more his.

"Get me another beer from the fridge would you, love? Bloody piss poor excuse for a referee is doing my head in." He reached for me and patted my bottom.

"Make me a sandwich too, will you? There's a good girl."

"I'm not a girl."

"Nooo! That's got to be offside! Come on ref!" He slurped his beer. "What did you say, love?"

"I'm not a girl," I replied, but he was more interested in the little red and white shirts running about on the TV.

"I'll have that roast ham I got from the market, okay?"

"What? You bought ham? You know damn well I'll have no pig meat in this house."

"Sorry love, I'd forgotten but it is organic and local. Try some."

"I'm vegetarian you idiot."

"Goal! Yes. That's more like it. Come on reds."

Passing into the kitchen I noticed the heavy cast iron frying pan I used for roasting chestnuts was not in its usual place. I loved roasting chestnuts all alone by the fire in winter with the wild pigs rustling outside. Sighing, I silently cursed Rob for not putting it back where I kept it and brushed my fingers over the cold metal feeling its solidity.

"Hurry up with that beer!"

My fingers quivered.

"Actually put a few in the ice bucket, save me having to get up again."

"You haven't gotten up once," I replied, my fingers curling around the handle.

"I'll have some cheese with that ham sandwich, too."

The handle felt a little greasy – had he used it to cook meat in, I wondered? I picked it up and carried it through to the living room.

"Have you been using my special chestnut pan to cook meat?" I queried.

"Go on son…Yes! Well played. We may win this, love."

I sniffed the handle, then the pan itself and the faintest stench of bacon lingered. He must have done it whilst I was out walking the other day. With the doors and windows open I hadn't smelt anything, but I remembered asking him why he was burning incense. Breathing in, like I did before a yoga movement, I raised the heavy pan high in the air. Shifting my grip, I relished the hefty weight and brought it down with all my might across the side of his head. I have no idea where I got the strength or the guts to do such a thing. I suppose you could say he drove me to it, pushed me over the edge, just like Daddy when he'd forced bacon into my mouth.

At first, I was terrified, afraid he would jump up and bash me back – but he didn't. Instead, he slowly slumped to the side. In a panic I checked his pulse and much to my amazement he didn't have one, not anymore anyway. Carefully I carried the pan into the kitchen and put it to soak in some hot water and washing up liquid. By the noise coming from the TV it sounded like Rob's favourite team had won the game. I smiled as I went back into the living room and saw the red shirts running around like crazy hugging each other. Turning off the TV, I tidied away the empty beer cans and began making my house mine again.

The only problem was Rob. His great big hulk still sat slumped in the chair. I hadn't planned on doing what I'd done, and half of me still expected him to get up and begin shouting at me for hitting him. I refilled my drink and made myself a salad sandwich, throwing that terrible ham into the bin. How dare he, I thought, I'll bloody show him, and then I remembered he'd never be able to do it again. This left me feeling strangely relieved. I sat down on the terrace to eat my sandwich, relishing the newfound peace and quiet. The sow and her piglets returned to feed.

Now I know what you're thinking, and you'd be right. Daddy had given me the idea when I'd found Mummy's wedding ring in the pig swill. He'd followed in pretty much the same way. The Tamworths had been my friends and partners in crime so to speak. Now it was the wild boars' turn. I struggled to drag Rob outside. He wasn't the lightest of men, but I'd managed it before any serious leakage had spoiled my chair and floor. Then I stripped him, placing his clothes into the log burner for when the chill night air moved in. The rest of his stuff I'd bag up and give away to charity. There were plenty of homeless on the streets of the larger French cities who would appreciate Rob's wardrobe.

I spent most of the evening watching the boars devour Rob's pale lumpy body. Quite a few of them came out of the woods that night. I did chuckle when his head rolled aside like a football. A large male took a fancy and snuffled it away from the others claiming it and dribbled it amongst the roots like a pro. Rob told me once that I had pigs on the brain. How funny it was to see that big snout dislodge Rob's lower jawbone, and snuffle and slurp inside his skull. Now who had pigs on the brain!

It took a few more nights for the boars to clear away all the remains. Other animals also scavenged, foxes probably took some of the larger bones and a couple of stray cats joined the banquet. What was left of the skull I buried in a deep hole, along with the ham I removed from the bin, and above it I planted a white pine of Provence. That way at Christmas I could put lights in the tree. I'd raise a toast to Rob, and the poor pig he was senselessly prepared to eat and celebrate the life I'd reclaimed for myself and my beautiful wild boar.

That was a couple of weeks ago and I feel like a new woman already. Even my precious boar seem happier – well, they'd had a prime feast to get through. I'd begun snuffling about in the woods myself lately. It felt comfortable and somehow familiar joining them instead of just watching. The autumn evenings were still quite mild and there was no one to see me so I started removing my clothes and rolling about in the beasty smelling earth. I delighted in watching my pale skin bristle and brown and relished the feel of damp leaf mulch sliding between my buttocks. My ginger hairs looked very much like the old Tamworth's as they caught the evening sun.

I'd started eating the mushrooms raw which the boar favoured, and had recently eaten the acorns too, mixing them up with the chestnuts. I'd broken two front teeth cracking the outer shells to reach the bitter insides. The boar joined me every evening and it seemed easier to copy them and use my face to root about in the earth. I'd always had a big nose, Mummy and Daddy had teased me relentlessly about it. Even the kids at school had called me Miss Piggy.

I snorted a giggle as I wallowed in a muddy patch the old sow had made, her piglets joining me squealing with delight. I smiled feeling their little bodies wriggling and snuffling my naked breasts, snouts all warm and wet. Maybe I'd follow the boars back to their leafy dens and sleep in the forest from now on. They'd accepted me. I was part of the family.

Author note: I used to live in a forested region in the South of France and spent some time in the Alentejo of Portugal. In both places I saw many wild boars rooting and snuffling around in the cork oak woodlands; they frightened me but were also fascinatingly beautiful animals. I like to think of my character in this story as enjoying her freedom from human 'swine' and breaking away from her humanity, while embracing the inner beast to wallow in the earth with her swine brethren. In fact, I almost envy her freedom and uninhibited beastliness. This too was first published online in a journal sadly no longer available, so read it here folks before the wild boar get to it!

## The End

# About the Author
# Julie Ann Rees

Julie Ann Rees has a PhD in creative writing from Swansea university and an MA from the University of Wales Trinity Saint David. She is a single mother to a talented grown up daughter and when not reading, writing or cuddling her fluffy gray cat Griffin, she can be found walking in the wild or riding her horse, Chi. She lives near Swansea in South Wales and works full time as a university library assistant.

## Also by Julie Rees
## Paper Horses

ISBN: 978-1-913853-09-9 (eBook)
ISBN: 978-1-913853-08-2 (Paperback)

"Brave, powerful and impossible to put down, Paper Horses is an important memoir of surviving coercive control" – Western Mail

When Julie Rees met her handsome and sophisticated French boyfriend, she thought her life had taken a fairy-tale turn. Moving to the South of France with him and her horses to set up a trail-riding business seemed like a dream come true.

And then it all turned sour. Gradually, Julie discovered that her Perfect Prince was in fact a Troll. Through social isolation, devastating bush fires and even a spell in a French jail, Paper Horses paints a raw and honest portrayal of life in a psychologically abusive relationship, and how the love for her child and her horses gave Julie the strength to survive.

At times painful, always inspiring, this memoir details how easy it is to be drawn into an abusive relationship, and how the love of and for others can not only help you escape, but thrive.

# Also from Black Bee Books
# Arianwen
## by Angela Johnson

ISBN: 978-1-913853-01-3 (eBook)
ISBN: 978-1-913853-00-6 (Paperback)

Born in a hidden valley in West Wales during the first half of the 20th century, Arianwen is one of the blessed: one to whom life comes easily.

Hers is an ordinary life, similar to the lives we all live, filled with the small pleasures that help us bear life's little tragedies, in the hope things will get better again.

But in a fast-changing world, Arianwen must learn the hard way. It is endurance that will see her through real adversity.

Elegantly written with an understated humour and a lyricism that reflects the natural rhythms of the Welsh language, Arianwen is the captivating portrait of one woman who represents us all.

# And: a memoir of my mother
## by Isabel Adonis
## Winner Creative Nonfiction, Wales Book of the Year Award 2023

ISBN: 978-1-913853-11-2 (eBook)
ISBN: 978-1-913853-10-5 (Paperback)

Simultaneously personal and universal, and told in the rhythms of an oral story, this beautifully musical and multi-layered book examines the divisiveness of colour, alienation, the impact of colonialism on social culture, and what it means to be 'mixed'.

Isabel Adonis was born in London in 1951, to Welshwoman Catherine Alice Hughes, and renowned Guyanese artist Denis Williams, whose work has been exhibited in the Tate Gallery.

Growing up in London, Sudan and Wales, with a cold and distant father and an isolated mother, Adonis explores the nature of identity, culture and desire as shaped by her childhood impressions of her parents.

An essential read that portrays an important aspect of the culturally diverse social fabric of Wales and the wider world.

### Reviews
Nation.Cymru: "…an extraordinary narrative, a swirling and circling story of language and heroism."

The Cardiff Review: "Stylistically, Adonis' prose calls to mind the kind of oral storytelling found in the Bible, or Homer."

The Western Mail: "…an intense, hypnotic read. Adonis' writing is keenly observant, and sometimes incantatory in its rhythm and repetition.

Paul Theroux: "I admire this book - a family entangled in Wales and the West Indies and Africa - a dominant father casting his shadow over the narrative. It is a complex memoir, related in a quiet and incantatory way, for which the word "Faulknerian" is not an exaggeration. It is in many ways a dark tale, but its heart and its humanity gives it great power."

Jim Perrin: "…the freshest, most exquisitely written, most observant, complex and insightful cultural memoir ever written about growing up in North Wales. I thoroughly recommend it to you."